ONE OF THE BOYS

"The party was fun, wasn't it," Jason said. He pulled me closer to him, and brought his face down to mine for a good night kiss.

As his warm lips covered mine, I pulled back, not at all interested. "It was fun," I agreed. "But it's late so I think I'll go in now."

"I guess it is late," Jason admitted, stepping back calmly. "See you at practice, Jenny."

I opened the front door and went inside, hot tears of disappointment streaming down my face. The evening had not turned out the way I'd expected it would at all.

Why should I have to kiss cute but incredibly boring Jason? Especially when I wanted to be kissing Rick Henley.

Bantam Sweet Dreams Romances
Ask your bookseller for the books you have missed

One of the Boys

Jill Jarnow

BANTAM BOOKS
TORONTO · NEW YORK · LONDON · SYDNEY · AUCKLAND

RL 6, IL age 11 and up

ONE OF THE BOYS
A Bantam Book / April 1986

Cover photo by Pat Hill.

ISBN 0-553-25536-3

Published simultaneously in the United States and Canada

Bantam Books are published by Bantam Books, Inc. Its trademark, consisting of the words "Bantam Books" and the portrayal of a rooster, is Registered in U.S. Patent and Trademark Office and in other countries. Marca Registrada. Bantam Books, Inc., 666 Fifth Avenue, New York, New York 10103.

PRINTED IN THE UNITED STATES OF AMERICA

O   0 9 8 7 6 5 4 3 2 1

One of the Boys

Chapter One

I was sitting peacefully at the desk in my room, trying to memorize French verbs that were bound to be on the next day's quiz, when my brother Roger burst in and threw himself down on my bed.

"This day will go down in history as the end of the North Hollow varsity soccer team," he announced bitterly. He was wearing his practice shorts, shirt, and grass-stained knee pads. "I can see the headlines now," he continued, " 'Champs for Five Years Destroyed in One Week.' "

"Roger, what are you talking about?" I asked, without looking up from my notes.

"Oh, don't let me bother you," he said sarcastically. "Homework is more important than varsity soccer."

"Well, I *am* having a test tomorrow," I answered defensively, glancing up at him.

1

Roger, who is two years older than I, is a senior at North Hollow High. He's tall and wiry, with brown, curly hair and green eyes. I think he's really cute—even though he is my brother. We've always been good friends.

"Sorry, Jenny," he said. "I have to talk to someone. Remember last week when we found out that the Anderson twins were moving away?"

I nodded my head. It would be hard to forget how miserable Roger had been when he learned that their best backfielders were moving to Texas.

"Well, if that wasn't bad enough, get this— Benjy Linker is being suspended from the team because of his grades."

"But, Roger, he's only the manager," I reminded him.

"Jenny, not just the manager. Aside from being a really great guy, he's fabulous at getting things done." Roger was really agitated.

"Don't you think you're getting a little carried away?"

"No, and you won't think so either when you hear who Coach Willens *might* put in for him. Bert Richmond!"

"What's wrong with him?" I asked. "Wasn't he vice-president of your class last year?"

"Yes, and if he does this job anything like he did that one, we're in big trouble. We almost didn't have a junior picnic because of him. He only wants the soccer job because it'll look good on his college applications. Soccer means nothing to him."

I did understand Roger's feelings of anger and frustration. We had both loved soccer since elementary school. I had been on a team, too, until last year when we moved to North Hollow from Harbor Heights. They're only twenty miles away from each other on Long Island, but their attitudes about soccer are entirely different.

After years of dreaming about having a business of their own, my parents had bought a real estate agency in North Hollow. Actually, I really liked our new town and my new school. My only major complaint was that there was no soccer team for me to play on, not even an independent team that wasn't part of the school. Girls in North Hollow just didn't play soccer.

Roger was still sprawled out on my bed, and I was studying my page of verbs when Dad called, "I could use a table setter down here. Dinner will be ready in twenty minutes." Dad does most of the cooking in our house while

Roger, my little sister Erin, Mom, and I set the table and clean up.

"Roger, would you do it tonight?" I asked. "It's really my turn, but I could use the extra time on my French."

"Yeah, I guess so," he answered, dragging himself off the bed.

"You're a pal," I told him. "If there's ever anything I can do for you, just let me know."

Mom arrived home from the office just in time to eat. "Dinner smells great," she yelled. I heard her briefcase land on the table by the front door. Then she came into the dining room to join us.

She always looked so nice in the morning, but now, at the end of the day, her navy suit and pink silk blouse were slightly rumpled. Her stylish short brown hair was just a little out of place, and her eyes looked tired, but she had a smile on her face.

"What a terrific day it turned out to be," she told us.

She filled us in on the details as we ate Dad's macaroni and cheese.

"It was so quiet," she began, "that I had decided to come home a little early. But just as I was about to leave, several calls came in on the Hawkhurst property. You know, John," she told my father, "I think that ad you wrote for the Sunday magazine section is really going to pay off. And when it does, I'll know the agency is launched!" They exchanged quiet smiles.

They had been working really hard, but they were still waiting for their big break.

"I'm glad somebody had a good day," Roger said, "because I sure didn't." Roger had taken a shower since I had last seen him. He was wearing clean jeans, a clean shirt, and his hair was soaking wet.

"What happened, Rog?" Dad wanted to know. Dad and Roger could look like brothers if Dad's curly hair wasn't streaked with gray. Both Mom and Dad stayed young and active by running and swimming.

Roger retold the story of what he considered to be the demise of his championship soccer team.

"Sounds bad," Dad agreed, between bites of salad. "And you've worked so hard this season. I know it hasn't been easy."

"Yeah!" Roger said. "And now we're not only losing Benjy, but we're getting the world's most unreliable person as his replacement."

"It's hard to believe Willens would do something like that on purpose," said Mom.

"I suppose it's hard to get a good soccer

manager at a moment's notice," Roger conceded. "Everyone who loves the game is busy playing on the team. Besides, I don't think he knows what Bert Richmond is really like."

"What does the job entail?" Mom wanted to know.

"A lot of stuff, really," Roger said. "Getting all the equipment organized for practices, arranging transportation for away games, getting stuff ready for home games, being at all the games, and keeping the statistics. Anyone could do the job, but the right manager would be someone who really loves soccer, who cares if we win, and who knows what to say when the chips are down."

"I can think of someone who fits the bill perfectly," said Dad in an instant. "And that person is sitting right at this table."

"Me!" exclaimed Erin. "I'm perfect." She's ten, skinny, with short, curly brown hair and freckles, sort of a miniature girl version of Dad and Roger.

"Dad, you can't be serious?" demanded Roger.

"I wasn't thinking of Erin," he admitted with a smile. "Not for this year, anyway. And your mother and I have more than we can handle at the office."

"You were thinking of Jenny?" Roger seemed surprised.

"Why not? She knows more about soccer than most people, and I suspect she plays a lot better than some of the boys on the team."

"That's true," my brother agreed quietly.

"Are you afraid there would be some objection to Jenny being manager because she's a girl?" Mom wanted to know.

"No, I just never thought about it before. But now that you mention it, Jenny would be perfect. Not only is she one hundred percent reliable, but a lot of the guys on the team already know what an ace she is."

He was quiet for a second, deep in thought. Then he said, "You know, the more I think about it, the more I realize you would be the perfect soccer manager, Jen." His voice had suddenly become excited. "In fact, you'd be dynamite!"

"Wait a minute," I told him, trying hard to be the voice of reason. "Aren't you going a little too fast here? Nobody even said I could have the job." I was definitely intrigued.

"Are you kidding? If Willens knew you were interested, he'd offer it to you in a second. So, what do you say?"

"Well," I said, hesitating, "I suppose I could

7

do it, but he wouldn't give it to me over Bert Richmond."

"Don't worry," Roger assured me. "When the team hears you're available, they'll convince Willens to give it to you. You've always been friendly with the guys on the team."

After dinner was cleaned up, I went back to my room to finish studying French. When I felt confident the verbs would stay in my mind, at least through sixth period the next day, I let my thoughts wander to soccer.

I didn't want to get too excited about being soccer manager because it seemed like such a long shot. But it was something I could really get into. I loved soccer, and I missed playing it. If there was no team for me to play on, managing Roger's team would be almost as good. *Better put it out of my mind*, I told myself. *It probably won't happen.*

Stiff from sitting at my desk, I got up and started pacing around my room. I began to think about myself and the way I looked to other people.

I take after my mom, so I'm small, just a couple of inches over five feet. And although I'm thin, I'm not super skinny like Roger and Erin. My brown eyes and turned-up nose are a lot like my brother's and sister's. But they have nice curls; my brown hair doesn't curl,

8

and it doesn't stay straight. So I just let it grow and wear it pulled back in a ponytail. It's not the height of fashion, but it takes no time at all to make, and then I never have to worry about it.

I think of myself as easygoing with a cute face and a lot of energy. I'd fit in with any soccer team. In fact, since we had moved to North Hollow, I had spent a lot of time with Roger and his soccer buddies.

The Sunday afternoon right after we had moved and Roger had just made the team, two of the guys from the Arrows team arrived at our house on their bikes.

"We were out cruising and thought you might like to join us," said Ted Stark. "We're going to the doughnut shop downtown." He had a sturdy, medium-height build, dark blond hair, and bright blue eyes.

Roger and I had been kicking the soccer ball around in the backyard. "Sounds great," agreed Roger. "Except my sister and I were just—" he started to explain as if he were unsure about how they'd react to me.

"Hey, do you both have bikes?" asked Matt Schmidt. "The more, the merrier." He was tall and skinny like my brother, with white blond hair and eyebrows.

"Coming right up," answered Roger as the two of us disappeared into the garage.

It took half an hour to reach Uncle Benny's Donut Factory. It was all uphill, but a fun trip. We slowed down each time we passed what Ted or Matt considered one of the important spots in town: the best pizza shop, the best sports shop, the best pier for fishing, and the short cut to school.

When we finally reached Uncle Benny's, we bought a tray of doughnuts in assorted flavors and four huge cups of milk. We sat down at a round table to pig out.

"I'm going to cut these little babies into quarters," announced Matt. "Unless anyone has any serious objections. This was we can all get a taste of everything. Then we can vote on our favorites."

"This I have to see," I said.

"Are you saying I can't do it?" he asked with a smile.

"No," I assured him. "But you're about to be in goo up to your elbows."

"Watch and weep," he boasted as he cut into his first doughnut and jelly squirted on his hand.

All four of us laughed.

"That was a plot to hog all the raspberry

jelly, Schmidt," accused Ted. "Now we're going to have to taste-test your fingers."

After that afternoon Ted, Matt, and some of the other guys from the team would drop by our house a lot. Sometimes we would go on bike rides or to the movies, but mostly we would just hang out together, kicking a soccer ball around the yard or watching sports shows on TV.

My parents had always made our friends feel welcome at our house, so it was natural that everyone liked to spend time there. No one ever minded that I was around. Now, I might have an official reason to hang out with them. I couldn't think of anything more fun than being manager of the soccer team, except of course, getting to play on it.

Chapter Two

Morning in our house is a real scene. Everybody gets up and going at his or her own speed. Eventually we all meet in the kitchen in various states of alertness. Although Roger and I have to be out first, Dad usually gets up earliest to go running. He gets back just as I get to the kitchen, with Roger dragging in a few minutes behind me.

Erin and Mom get up after we do. Erin's school starts an hour later than the high school, and she and Mom usually wander down to the kitchen in their bathrobes, happy but groggy as they bang around and make breakfast together.

That next morning I had showered and pulled on a reasonably new pair of jeans and a navy blue T-shirt that said Cornell in red letters before I went to the kitchen. I ate my breakfast slowly, sitting on a stool at the counter while Roger uncharacteristically bolted down his Cheerios and banana.

"I'm running over to school," he told me between gulps, "to see if I can catch Willens before homeroom. I want to find him before he talks to Bert."

"Don't drive yourself crazy on my account," I said. "Managing the team would be fun, but it won't be the end of the world if I don't get it."

"Yeah, but it may well be the end of the North Hollow Arrows if you don't!"

I'll never know exactly what he said to Coach Willens, but when Roger found me in the lunchroom at school a few hours later, he had a big grin across his freckled face, and his green eyes were sparkling. He gave me a thumbs-up sign and then patted me on the back.

"We're in business," he told me. "Coach gave you the go ahead, and he wants to talk to you before practice today."

"No kidding, Roger? That's great," I said.

"So I'll meet you in the gym at a quarter to three, sport." With that, he headed for the lunch line.

I was sitting at a table eating lunch with my two best girl-friends, Gretchen and Amy. They were both in my grade, and we had some of the

13

same classes. I liked being with them, but I couldn't get into talking about clothes and boys the way they did.

"Jenny, your brother gets cuter every day," Gretchen said as soon as Roger was out of ear-shot. She's a few inches taller than I am and sturdy. She has a round, wholesome face and shoulder-length straight blond hair that always falls just right.

"And he's so nice," added Amy. She was taller than Gretchen, slender, with short, sleek black hair. She gets up every morning at five to swim on the team. I had thought about trying out, but I'm too slow in the water. Amy has admitted that though she may swim like a shark, on dry land she feels out of place.

Gretchen, who has no interest in sports, has a beautiful voice and is saving up her baby-sitting money to take singing lessons in New York City.

What the three of us really have in common is our love of music oldies.

Gretchen and I met at a neighborhood garage sale. We were both checking through a pile of albums. I was looking to see if there were any real collectors' items, such as the Beatles' *Yesterday And Today*.

At first we were really suspicious of each

other, but we started talking as we poked through the piles.

"Are you looking for something special?" she asked.

"Not really," I admitted. "Anything from the fifties or sixties."

"There's an *Abbey Road* in the carton next to this," she said. "I've got it already, and it's really terrific."

"Hey, thanks," I said, appreciating the information. "I love it, too, but my copy is all scratched up. Maybe this one will be in better condition."

It didn't take us long to realize that it would be more fun to be friends than competitors. Gretchen was so easy to talk to and so devoted to the Beatles that within five minutes I knew I wanted to be her friend. It turned out that we lived a few houses from each other, too.

It was hard for me to get to know Amy, though. She collected Beatles records and memorabilia, too, but she was not so willing to be my friend at first. I think it was because she thought I might come between her and Gretchen.

I tried to make it obvious that since I was new in North Hollow, I would rather have two new friends than one. Also, I was totally in awe of her swimming ability and told her so. Eventually she warmed up, and the three of us spent time talking rock 'n' roll trivia and hunting for records and other collectibles.

Also the three of us were very serious about doing well in school. Since we had a lot of the same classes, we often did our homework together, compared notes, and studied together for tests.

The last spring, when I had first moved to North Hollow, we did a presentation together for government class on the judicial system. Gretchen was a whiz at organizing, Amy loved doing research, and I got involved in making elaborate charts and diagrams to highlight our project. We were the only group that got an A, and it made us feel great.

There were also times that we spent talking about clothes and boys. Sometimes I had to laugh though, especially when they picked out a boy who they thought was really cute, and he turned out to be one of my brother's soccer friends. When they finally noticed Roger, I had to admit I was really amused.

"Is Roger going with anyone right now?" Gretchen asked.

"You picked the wrong one this time," I said as I laughed. "My brother has only one thing on his mind, and that's soccer. He hasn't been out with a girl in his life."

"You Millers," she complained good-naturedly. "You're no fun at all." Gretchen, for all her talk, had been out with only one guy, and she had certainly never dated him steadily.

"But soccer is a lot of fun," I told her.

"Maybe for guys," said Amy.

"Come on, Amy. It's a great sport for girls," I answered. "In Harbor Heights we had a terrific girls' team. What's with this place, anyway?"

"Let's face it," said Amy. "The football field gets resurfaced every season while we hold our breath for new goggles for the swim team. As for soccer, they're lucky to even have a boys' team. North Hollow is really a football town."

"I really miss soccer," I told them. "But it looks like I'm at least going to be able to manage Roger's team."

"It would drive me crazy to manage the swim team and not be able to swim," said Amy.

I shrugged my shoulders. "Maybe I'll get to kick the ball around with the guys a little. It'll be better than nothing."

"Now, Amy, you're forgetting something very important," Gretchen reminded her. "Jenny gets to be with all those adorable guys on the team."

"They are awfully cute," agreed Amy.

But I could only groan. "Grow up, you two. There's more to life than cute boys."

"Right," said Gretchen. "*Dates* with cute boys."

The afternoon went smoothly. I was pretty sure I had gotten an A on the French quiz. Madame had chosen exactly the verbs I had studied the night before. But as I double-checked my endings, I began to feel a tightness in my stomach that had nothing to do with French verbs.

I started to think about soccer. What if Roger was wrong? What if Coach Willens decided to give the job to Bert Richmond after all? Or what if someone else more qualified than I was had come along?

When the bell rang, I handed in my test and flew to the girls' room, where I scrubbed my hands and face and made sure my T-shirt and jeans were reasonably neat and clean. I even brushed out my hair and pinned it back again in barrettes. I wanted to look as together and responsible as possible.

I got to the gym a little early. A custodian, changing a light bulb, was standing on a huge ladder at one end. At the other end a few guys were shooting baskets, their voices echoing across the room.

As I sat in the bleachers watching them, I began to feel more and more nervous and out of place. Again I started to doubt that I was the perfect manager. Then I began to worry that my brother had totally misunderstood Coach Willens's decision.

I was fidgeting with my books when Roger wandered in a few minutes later. Sitting down next to me, he tossed a pile of books on the wooden bleacher seat.

"Coach here yet?" he asked.

"I haven't seen him."

"Well, don't worry. He said he might be a little late. He had a meeting with Mr. Sandowsky."

"The vice-principal?"

Roger nodded.

My mind was racing now. "You don't suppose he's checking up on me or something?" I whispered.

"What if he is? You've never been in trouble, have you? Your grades are OK, aren't they?"

"Yes," I had to agree.

"So relax, Jen. Everything is going to be just fine."

Coach Willens arrived a few minutes later. He was a short, powerful-looking man in his forties with a full face and a bald head edged with a fringe of sandy-colored hair. He wore gray North Hollow sweats and walked briskly. Though he had a gruff manner, I knew that he was well liked and respected by the team.

"Miller," he said to Roger.

"Coach, this is my sister Jenny."

"Welcome," said Coach Willens in his deep voice, extending his hand to me. It was a firm handshake, and I did my best to return it in kind. "I was just at the front office checking out team rules and regulations," he told us.

I breathed deeply. It was impossible to tell from his expression what he was going to say next.

"From what I can see, the requirements for a varsity athletics team manager are that the person be a high-school student and in good academic standing, which Mr. Sandowsky tells me you are, Jenny. There's nothing to specify that the person be a boy or girl, and I'm embarrassed to say it's never come up before. Roger, my lad, you could even manage the girls' soccer team."

"If we had one," said Roger.

"Someday," promised the coach, though his voice sounded resigned to the idea that that "someday" was far in the future. "Besides, Miller, we need you on the boys' team. Meantime, Jenny, I hear from your brother that you're the person we need, and I'm delighted to take his recommendation."

"Thank you," I answered, feeling suddenly shy.

He smiled. "Today I was confronted by no less than ten of our boys, each putting in a good word for you. I'm relieved that everything checked out in the office. Until Roger gave me your name, Bert Richmond was the most qualified of our applicants, but there was little enthusiasm for him among the team members. That had me worried. If you hadn't been qualified, Jenny Miller, I think there might have been a mutiny around here."

I was smiling, and I could feel myself relax. "I'm really excited about it," I admitted. "And I'm so glad it worked out."

"Have you ever managed a team before?"

"No, but I played with the league when we lived in Harbor Heights. There was never an official manager, so we all chipped in to get things done. I'm sure if you show me how you do things here, I'll pick it right up."

Coach Willens pointed out the storerooms in the gym and promised to give me keys for the equipment shed and the linen closet.

"You'll have to keep careful watch over them, Jenny," he warned. "With our shaky budget, we can't afford to replace anything that gets filched."

"Different story if we were playing football, right, Coach?" put in Roger. I could see that this was a sore subject with Coach Willens.

"Miller, don't you have warm-ups in five minutes?"

"Yes, sir."

"Well, why don't you get changed?"

"Yes, sir."

"And, Miller," he added, "thanks a lot for recommending Jenny."

As Roger disappeared into the locker room, the coach turned to me. "And thank you, ahead of time, Jenny. The boys are very excited that you're joining us. And I can tell you they need a lift right now. North Hollow has had an undefeated team for the last few years, but the boys who were the backbone of the team graduated last June. These boys have it in them to win, make no mistake about that, but they've had their share of hard knocks lately."

"Like losing the Andersons?" I asked.

"Yes, for starters, and then they bombed in both their scrimmages. Now they've lost two games that weren't conference games. They have won their only league match, so it's not too late for them to win the league. But they've got to go for it. Attitude is a big part of the game here. Losing Benjy was the last thing they needed. Finding a good manager mid-September is difficult under any condition, but finding someone the boys feel good about is more than I could have expected."

"I'm glad to have the chance to do it," I told him. "I always hit the ball around with the guys when they hang out at our house, and we get along great."

"I can tell. And as far as I'm concerned, a coach can never have too many Millers."

He put me right to work assembling the equipment to carry out to the field for practice. As I pulled balls and cones from the storage shed in the gym, the boys were starting to trickle out of the locker room.

"Hey, Jenny, I heard you might be here," said Ted.

I was already carrying one of the cumbersome ball bags, and he came over and picked up the bag with the cones.

"Thanks a lot," I told him as we headed toward the door to the field. Leaning against the bar to open it with my arm, I heard from across the room, "Hold the door, you guys." Looking up, I saw Matt Schmidt and Nicky Esposito coming toward us. Matt had the rest of the cones in his arms, and Nicky was carrying the box with the goalie pads and headgear.

"H-e-l-l-o, Jenny," Matt said.

"Are we ever glad to see you, Miller," added Nicky, poking his head out from behind his pile of stuff.

We laughed together as we held the door open for one another. None of us had a free hand.

"You really know how to make a person feel welcome," I told them.

"Hey," said Ted. "What are friends for?"

Chapter Three

From the beginning I always took care of my manager duties first, and then I would join in with the guys while they did warm-up exercises and jog and sprint laps.

Though the coach never said anything, I could tell he was pretty surprised at my interest and ability, especially when he saw that I could keep up with the guys out on the field. It also helped that I have always been a good runner.

I run with Dad and Roger on weekends and by myself afternoons. As a result, I had no trouble running with the varsity soccer team. In fact, I had better endurance than a few of the guys.

With the Andersons having moved away and fall flu season taking its toll, we were inevitably short of players at practice. One day, when attendance was unusually low, the coach asked me to fill in by pairing off with Ted while we did foot-leg control drills. I did so well that Willens began to rely on me again and again. Because I hadn't played in a while, my timing was a bit off at first, but I was back in shape in just a few days.

The coach insisted that the team drill in different pairs at each practice so everybody would get used to working with everybody else. Since that first day when I had worked out with Ted, he asked me to fill in whenever there was an uneven number. As it turned out, I got to practice almost every day, and I loved it.

There were, of course, a couple of the guys I didn't know at all. One was Jason Tremain, and another was Rick Henley. They hung around together, separate from Roger's crowd. They were really good players, and they were also really cute. Eventually I had to practice with each of them.

When it was Jason's turn to drill, there was no joking around. There wasn't even a hello. We just got right to work. I began by lobbing the ball to him, and he headed it back to me. The idea was to keep the ball off the ground as long as we could using only our heads. I could tell he was surprised at my ability to keep up the volley.

When we were done, he looked overheated and even more intense than when we had started.

"You are good," he conceded, breathing heavily and wiping his forehead on his sleeve.

"Great volley. You gave me a good run," I told him, short of breath myself.

"What did you say your name was?" he asked as if he had never seen me before.

"Jenny Miller. I'm Roger's sister."

"Should have known," he grunted and turned away.

It was Rick Henley's turn next, and he took one look at me and laughed. I must have been a pretty bedraggled sight with my dripping face, my washed-out sweat suit, and my unruly hair, neat a mere six hours earlier, now radiating in uncontrollable wisps around my head.

"Jenny Miller," he scoffed, showing me that he at least knew my name. "Coach has got to be kidding. How am I going to practice anything with you?"

Rick *was* a lot taller than I was, with muscular-looking legs. But then, I was wearing big baggy sweat clothes that probably made me look more fragile than I was.

"Look," I said quickly and with very little

patience. "We've got an uneven number, and Willens thinks it's better to practice in twos."

"Unbelievable," he said, snickering and looking incredibly cute in his green and white North Hollow shorts and sweat shirt. His face was strong and handsome with a creamy complexion, and he had the most enormous gray eyes fringed with thick, dark lashes. His hair was dark and wavy, and though he wasn't as tall as my stringbean of a brother, he was built a lot better with wider shoulders and more powerful-looking arms.

Because he had no expectations for my soccer playing being even halfway decent, I was determined to show him that I really could play. I was looking forward to seeing the exasperated expression on his face.

I concentrated on lofting the ball carelessly, but as Rick continued to stare at me, I realized that for the first time since I had become team manager, I was feeling self-conscious and uneasy.

It was an awful feeling. I couldn't imagine what had come over me. There were a lot of cute guys on the team, and not one of them made me feel as awkward as I felt at that moment.

"We'd better get started," he said with resignation, "or the coach will be on my case."

"OK, Mr. Superstar. Let's go." I said as I passed the ball to him higher than I intended.

Ordinarily I would have moved forward to meet the ball head on, but with a skeptical, gorgeous Rick facing me, I lost my rhythm. It was purely a case of nerves. In the process of calming myself down, I inadvertently let the ball go over my head. Rick had a smug, almost condescending look on his face. It was an unavoidable challenge, almost as if he were waving a red flag under my nose.

Suddenly I pulled myself together so that I could show him just what I could do. I let the volley start slowly, moving forward to head the ball easily back to him a few times. I wanted desperately to show my best stuff.

And I did. The ball went faster and faster as my returns went from easy lobs to long, low shots that I delivered by jumping to meet the ball. I knew I was giving Rick much more than he expected. I was making him work really hard to send the ball back, and by the time I finally stopped the ball with my foot, I could see he had revised his opinion of me.

As we stood facing each other, both dripping with sweat, he could only laugh. "Good show, Miller. I'll proceed to eat my hat. Now I know why there was such excitement about your becoming manager. And I thought it was just because you were such a cute kid."

I smiled grotesquely and batted my eyelashes at him in an attempt to look like the cute kid he thought he was describing. I absolutely detested being called a cute kid.

"I hope you will excuse my mistake," he said with sudden seriousness.

"Never," I said, clutching my heart and hoping to cover my mixed-up feelings with clowning.

"What are you doing here, anyway?" he asked.

"Roger volunteered me for manager when Benjy dropped out. I love soccer, and North Hollow has no girls' team, so it seemed like a good job for me."

"Your playing surprised me, I have to admit. Thanks for the workout," Rick said easily.

He ran off across the field to rejoin the team, leaving me feeling very unsettled. Talking to Rick was different from talking to any of the other guys. Was it just because I didn't know him? But then, I didn't know Jason either, and being with him hadn't undermined my self-confidence.

I was still deep in thought when the coach called the team together for a pep talk about the next day's game against Long Meadow. I gladly gathered up the equipment and hurried to store it away.

I wasn't in the mood to talk to anyone, but as I was locking up the equipment shed, Matt and another boy, Jeremy, insisted I go with them to Jo-Jos for a quick before-homework break. Suddenly, being with them seemed like a good idea. Matt and Jeremy were nice, comfortable boys, and that was what I wanted at the moment.

I had shown Rick Henley that I knew how to play soccer, and now he knew who I was. But I wasn't just some cute kid; I was a kid who knew the game. But was that the only thing I wanted him to know about me?

Chapter Four

In the next few weeks we won the game against Long Meadow and two more besides. I loved going to practice, and Gretchen and Amy were amazed at the change in me after I'd become manager.

"I like telling you jokes," Gretchen said one day as she, Amy, and I were sitting in the school commons waiting for lunch period to end. "It's so easy to make you laugh now."

"I feel good," I admitted. "It's great managing the soccer team."

Just then Ted and Nicky walked by.

"Hi, Jen," called out Nicky. "Ready for the big game tomorrow?"

"I am if you are," I answered back.

"Buses or car pool?" Matt wanted to know.

"Car pool for this one, bus for Whitman High on Friday."

"Want to be in my car?" asked Ted.

"Sure, why not?" I responded easily.

"Get out of here, Stark," cut in Nicky. "Jenny might want to be in my car."

Both boys had their own cars, which we depended on for some of the transportation. The school district allowed us money for buses to three away games, and this year we had five—so we had to fill in ourselves.

"Why don't we work it out at practice later," I suggested.

"OK," said Ted. "But promise you won't go with Henley. He always gets all the girls."

"Come on, guys. You know I'm not like that," I said.

"Catch you later, Jenny," said Nicky, and the two boys hurried through the huge, crowded hallway.

I turned back to Gretchen and Amy, who were both staring at me. They seemed shocked.

"You talk to them so easily," said Amy.

"They're just the guys on the soccer team. You forget we're really good friends."

"I'd like to be good friends like that," said Gretchen.

"Come over to my house any weekend and hang out with us," I replied.

"Really?" asked Gretchen. "What do you think, Amy?"

"They're so cute," she said.

"Ted and Nicky aren't the only cute ones," I told them, getting into the spirit of things. "You should see the rest of the team."

"Like your brother," said Amy with a sigh.

"Hey, I'll be there," said Gretchen. "So what if Saturday is my morning for dance class. I'll move it to some other day."

Later that afternoon at practice, I had to smile when I thought about Gretchen and Amy. They talked about getting "in" with the boys on the team, but for Matt, Ted, Nicky, Roger, and their friends, the world revolved around soccer. Without soccer, I couldn't imagine what they would have to say to one another.

But I had a dilemma of my own, one that had been constantly on my mind and one that I had admitted to no one. If I mentioned it to Amy and Gretchen, it would be their turn to laugh.

Since the week when I had first practiced with Rick Henley, my fascination with him had been growing. I couldn't believe what was happening to me. But instead of being able to talk myself out of it, my interest in Rick grew more and more intense.

I didn't just watch him in my spare minutes

at practice, I found myself watching *for* him all the time. It turned out that we passed each other in the hall a few times every day. "How are you doing, kid?" he'd say to me whenever we saw each other. Once in a while, he gave my hair a gentle tug.

Ordinarily that was the sort of behavior that would drive me right up a wall, but from Rick I could stand it. It meant he knew me, even though it was only fleeting recognition. His warm smile and gorgeous gray eyes stayed fixed in my mind as did the memory of the way he walked down the hall giving enthusiastic greetings to a lot of the people he passed.

I watched one day as Carol Kurtz, a spaced-out girl from my gym class, collided with Rick. It happened in the corridor between the third and fourth periods.

"Are you hurt?" he asked her patiently, though she was obviously at fault. He had managed to remain standing and hold on to his books. Carol, on the other hand, had ended up on the floor, her books scattered.

"I'm OK," she said vaguely. Rick had put down his books and gathered up hers.

"Well, I'd like to see your license and registration," he said in a good-natured voice. I smiled to myself.

"Uh, sure," mumbled Carol as she stood up,

grabbed her books from Rick, and hurried away without a word of apology. Rick just shrugged. He was so sweet about the whole thing.

It was still hard for me to believe that I could be so romantically interested in a boy, especially after all the time I had spent hanging out with Roger's friends. But Rick was different.

It wasn't just that he was cute. I knew a lot of good-looking guys. But to those great gray eyes and that dark, wavy hair were added a warmth and worldliness that made Rick Henley someone very special. I had never known anyone like him before. For the first time in my life, I wanted someone—I wanted Rick—to turn some of his easygoing attention toward me.

But the more I watched him, the more I realized I didn't have a chance. The trouble was that Stephanie Danworth, the queen of North Hollow High, stuck to him like glue.

A lot of girls, I'm sure, would have given anything to be in Stephanie's position. Amy and Gretchen had once made a comment about what a knockout Rick was, but dismissed him quickly as being unattainable. And they knew. They spent a lot of time studying this kind of thing.

But the more I watched Rick and the few

times I spoke to him at practice, the more I wanted to believe that Amy and Gretchen were wrong.

From studying Rick, I could see what kind of girl he liked. Stephanie and her crowd were very sophisticated, very different-looking from me in my crumpled any-old-thing-will-do clothes. If I was going to get Rick to notice me, I had to do something drastic. I was going to have to get my act together and make changes—*big* changes. I didn't want to look just nice, like Gretchen and Amy, but very polished, like Stephanie Danworth.

Stephanie was a lot different from Gretchen and Amy. Her short, sleek blond hair, tight pants, and oversize sweaters with belts, her carefully made-up face—everything she did or wore made her look as if she were posing for a fashion magazine. Amy and Gretchen, for all their talk, always managed to look more like real people than teenage superstars.

Not only did Stephanie stand out in a crowd, she somehow seemed to stand above it. She was the picture of glamour. And Stephanie's style and superior attitude were a complete mystery to me. But the more I watched, the more I decided that until I looked like Stephanie Danworth, I didn't have a chance with Rick.

It wasn't easy to try to figure out how to change myself from a fifteen-year-old girl-slob into a fifteen-year-old-super-sophisticate overnight. I didn't know where to start.

For one thing, Stephanie was tall and curvaceous with short cropped hair. She always wore big fashionable earrings. I was half her size with a more slender build and longer, dark hair. I had had my ears pierced when I was twelve because my best friend at the time had hers done, but I had always worn the same tiny gold posts.

I didn't know who to talk to. My mother always looked very pretty, in an older, professional way. I might have asked her for help, but she was preoccupied with big business deals. I figured she had enough on her mind.

Roger, who was really like a best friend to me, was absolutely useless in the style department. Dad wasn't much better. Erin, who was at least a girl, was just too young. Gretchen and Amy were certainly into clothes, but since I wanted to be a supersophisticate and not just a regular girl, I didn't even consider asking them for help. Not at first, anyway.

Instead, I armed myself with reference material: *Seventeen*, *Mademoiselle*, and *Glamour* magazines. Just buying them made me feel out of character, and I was glad the woman in the store put them in a paper bag for me, just in case I ran into someone I knew on the way home.

The magazines were chock full of articles about beauty make overs. Even though I had looked at pictures of clothes and hairstyles with Gretchen and Amy, I had never actually sat down with my very own magazines and looked at the specific articles. The more I turned the pages, the more I knew I was the only fifteen-year-old girl in the United States who had never read this stuff before. I was amazed at what I had been missing.

For three days I rushed through my homework and then spent the remainder of the evening poring over those glossy pages. And I read them in my room with the door shut.

After three days I was completely overwhelmed and I must have sounded extremely distressed when I called Gretchen on the phone because she ran all the way to my house and was banging on the door to my room about three minutes after we had hung up.

"What's the problem?" she asked, panting slightly.

"Nothing big," I assured her. "But I've decided to do a beauty make over on myself, and I'm not sure where to start."

"What is it that you want to make yourself

over into?" she asked narrowing her eyes. "It's going to be pretty hard for a person like you who hates to comb her hair and only wears scruffy jeans." After all the months of making fun of her and Amy, I had to forgive her sarcasm.

"I want to look like this," I told her as I held out the issue of *Glamour*. It was opened to a page with a girl dressed in cropped black and white checked pants, a big red sweater, and huge dangling earrings. She was tall and blond and looked suspiciously like Stephanie Danworth, complete with short blond hair and bright red lipstick.

"Great outfit," Gretchen admitted after a moment's glance. "But on you? Honestly, Jen. It hardly seems your style."

"But I want to make myself over," I explained again.

"It's going to be hard to hide your hair."

"I'm not opposed to cutting it off. In fact, I rather expect to."

"What!" It was obvious I had really shocked her. "Jenny, you sound serious."

"I am," I assured her.

"But why did you pick this model?"

"Because she looks the most like Stephanie Danworth," I told her honestly. "And since she's the most together-looking girl in school, she seems like a good person to copy."

"Except for the fact that you don't look anything like Stephanie, and you never will," Gretchen reminded me.

"It's her 'look' I'm after."

"Couldn't you choose something a little easier?" She didn't sound too optimistic.

"Will you help me?" I persisted.

"It's certainly a challenge," she said slowly. "Do you mind if we get Amy in on this? We could sure use another opinion."

"Fine," I agreed. "The sooner the better."

Chapter Five

Gretchen, Amy, and I agreed to be organized and formulate a plan before I did anything rash like cutting my hair or investing in a pair of dangly earrings. We spent as many hours as we could studying pictures in fashion magazines. Mom said she would be only too happy to let me use her charge cards, once I'd explained that I was ready for some "real" clothes. That was a huge help since I knew my own savings would go only so far.

The three of us spent Saturday morning exploring the shops at the North Hollow Mall. I tried on a lot of stuff with the idea that I was "just looking" for the time being. It was exciting to look at myself in the dressing room mirror wearing something really stylish. I looked completely different, so grown-up. But it was weird, too, because no matter how sophisticated I looked, I knew that underneath I was the same old me.

Over lunch we talked about everything I had tried on and made a list of what would match what. Then we went back to the stores, and I bought a lot of stuff.

Sunday morning Gretchen and Amy came over bright and early to look at everything we had chosen and to help me with my hair.

"There's so much you can do with it," Amy assured me as I sat in a chair in my room and she brushed it back and forth. She played around with different hair styles for more than half an hour. I still wasn't satisfied.

"It's just not what I had in mind," I told her.

"But your hair is so great," Gretchen said. "And cutting it is such a big step."

"I'm into it," I told them, and they eyed me warily.

Amy gave me the name of her haircutter, and I vowed to make an appointment as soon as possible.

Through all this, they never questioned me about what I was really thinking, about why I was suddenly so consumed with the desire to look so different.

"This is so much fun," said Gretchen as I modeled one of my new outfits, my hair in a french braid that she had just finished. "I knew it was just a matter of time before you got interested in the way you look," she added, pleased that she and Amy had finally converted me to a new and better way of life.

One of the nice things for Amy and Gretchen was that working on the "new me" meant that they were at my house a lot while Roger, Matt, and Nicky were hanging out. Even though I had suggested that they come over any time, they never had. For all their wisdom about boys, my two friends were chicken.

We spent most of the time huddled in my room, but inevitably we saw the boys in the kitchen when we went down for a snack. I was used to them, but Gretchen and Amy were suddenly transformed from chatty, bubbly friends into people I hardly knew. They became speechless!

Because they were my friends, Roger was perfectly willing to accept them. He had no idea that they were terror stricken in his presence.

"We were just going out for a run," he told us one day. "You guys want to come?"

"No, thanks, Rog," I answered. "I ran with Dad this morning."

"Either of you girls interested?" Roger asked nonchalantly.

"Uh, no thanks," mumbled Gretchen.

"Gee, I hardly ever run. I'm the slowest thing on two feet," admitted Amy, her voice filled with regret.

"Yes, but you swim miles," I reminded her.

"It's different," she said.

"If you want to come and take it really slow, we'll double back every few blocks and see how you're doing," offered Roger.

"If you don't mind—" she hesitated. "I've always wanted to give it a try."

So I lent Amy some shorts and an old pair of my running shoes that were a perfect fit. Giving Gretchen and me a big grin, she went out the door with the three boys.

"Wow," said Gretchen wistfully as the door shut behind them.

The two of us made a huge bowl of popcorn and looked through *Glamour* for the third time, discussing ways I might get my hair cut.

The runners were back in the kitchen forty-five minutes later. Hot and sweaty, looking like she was about to drop, Amy was still smiling.

"They lost me about one block into it," she said, laughing. "But I kept at it, at my own pace, and it really was fun. I might actually do it again one day."

"You could be good at it," Roger told her. "If

you break in slowly, you won't hurt yourself. And look what we found. It was on top of a junk pile over on Washington. I can't believe someone was throwing it out." He held up a big, fat paperback book with a tattered cover.

"It's *The Encyclopedia of Rock 'n' Roll*," Amy told us excitedly.

I watched Gretchen's mouth drop open as Amy and Roger sat down at the dining room table and started poring over the book. Seeing Amy and my brother chatting together so happily seemed to give her courage, and when Nicky and Matt asked if we wanted to play Trivial Pursuit, Gretchen was able to relax enough to get a few right answers. We played girls against boys, and neither team did very well, but we had a couple of good laughs together.

Gretchen and Amy helped me plan my outfit for the next day before they went home: a big lime green sweater with a black and yellow geometric design and black corduroy jeans. I went to bed that night full of high hopes.

In the morning when I got up, I put on my new clothes and braided my hair from a high ponytail, the way Amy had shown me. It took longer than I thought it would to get everything to look just right. By the time I went down to the kitchen, Roger and Dad had already left, and Erin and Mom were back in their rooms dressing. No one saw me when I left the house.

"Very nice," said Gretchen, and Amy nodded her approval when I met them in school.

"It's a start," I told them. "I meant to put on eye makeup, but it took so long to do my hair that I just didn't have time. And, of course, I still have to get my hair cut."

"Dr. Frankenstein, what have we created," said Gretchen, and we all laughed.

Though I was really excited about the way I looked, I discovered that I was going to have to transform the "new me" back into the "old me" to manage the soccer team. After working so hard to get myself together every day, I had to revert to my old after-school look.

The team was starting to come together. Mr. Willens had been emphasizing new field techniques, and the boys felt good about them because spirits were really high.

At practice Rick was glad to work out with me the way I did with Roger and his friends. But when I was with Rick, I became tongue-tied. At first I was horrified. Then I realized it was the same problem that afflicted Gretchen and Amy when they were around Roger and the other boys on the soccer team. I was encouraged when Amy began to make a miraculous recovery as she and Roger found more and more to talk about. They had even started talking to each other on the phone for a couple of evenings! It gave me hope that I wouldn't be a marble mouth forever.

When practice was over, Rick disappeared into the locker room. There he quickly changed and headed out to meet Stephanie. She was never far away.

I felt completely frustrated. I puttered around in the gym, putting gear in order so I could see him as he flew up the stairs and out the gym door. Knowing that he was going to pass by at any second, I searched my mind for something brilliant to say. But when the moment arrived, I found myself reduced to a mere "Bye, Rick" in my carefully casual tone. Inevitably, he would answer in his friendly way, "Bye, kid. Keep that ball rolling."

I had made a lot of changes in my appearance, but, somehow, my life seemed to have taken a giant step backward.

The week passed quickly, and soon it was Thursday, the day I had made an appointment to have my hair cut. I was really excited. I was also incredibly nervous. I had decided that once my hair was styled up around my ears, I would be a whole new person. Then Rick

Henley would surely realize I wasn't just a "kid."

He had been extra friendly at practice on Wednesday. He seemed only too pleased to help me with my footwork. "Don't forget you've got a left foot, squirt," he reminded me as we played around on the field before practice.

I usually hate being called names like that, but Rick meant it as a sign of friendship, and I couldn't reject that. As usual when practice was over, he vanished.

Thursday's practice was different because the next day was another league game. We wanted to win the league championship and keep up the North Hollow tradition. The coach felt we had a pretty good chance of winning. The varsity seemed to be getting itself together.

At the end of practice Mr. Willens got into a heavy, last-minute lecture with the boys. I put away the equipment and rushed out of the gym to keep my appointment with the haircutter.

I ran the whole way into town, and when I got there I was hot and sweaty, my hair frizzed around my face. Gretchen and Amy were waiting for me. Together with the haircutter they tried once more to talk me into a shoulder-

49

length haircut rather than the short, radical one I wanted. But I was firm. We spent ten minutes moving my hair around to study its natural wave, and talking about pictures of haircuts hanging all over the walls of the shop. John, the haircutter, understood what I wanted and set to work.

I had a pang of regret when he made the first cut, but seeing my hair lying in a pile on the floor wasn't as bad as it might have been. I was looking forward to the totally new me. I really did feel that my comfortable old braid was what lay between Rick and me, and I was only too happy to see it go.

I got what I wanted. My face looked so different when John was done, so much older and prettier. When my hair had been long, the weight of the ponytail had made it pretty straight. Now, it was much curlier and framed my face. I could hardly believe I was the same person. My head felt so light I wondered if it was still there.

Not only were Gretchen and Amy amazed, but everyone who saw me was momentarily speechless. I had told my mother what I was planning to do, but no one else knew.

She gave me a big kiss when I got home, and her eyes filled with tears.

"Don't mind me," she apologized. "You look

beautiful, Jen. It's just a shock for me to see my daughter look so grown-up." Dad and Roger were completely startled, and Erin wanted to run out before dinner and have her hair cut just like mine.

A lot of people, including Matt and Nicky, were shocked, but they told me I looked great. Everyone noticed except the most important person.

The next afternoon at the game I was dressed in some of my new clothes: a big turquoise sweater, cropped black pants, and black flats. Sitting at the folding table keeping the stats of the game, I realized that I looked like a completely different person.

I felt good anticipating some sort of a reaction from Rick, but at halftime, when he finally got around to making a comment, it was, "Hey, squirt, where's your nice ponytail?" Overcome with disappointment and fury, I could only muster up a grunt in response.

But there was an interesting sidelight. Rick Henley may have been completely unaffected by the way I looked, but Jason Tremain was not.

After the game, in which he and Rick scored all four of the winning goals, Jason went out of his way to talk to me for the first time.

"Great game," he said as we headed back to the gym for post-game snacks. "Nothing like a good, clean win. All we needed was for Willens to whip those younger kids into shape."

"You guys are looking really good," I agreed.

"Thanks. So are you. I like the way kid sisters grow up. Maybe there's some hope for mine," he said. I couldn't help but smile. "So, listen, has anyone asked you to the Harvest Moon Dance tomorrow?"

"Gee, no. I forgot all about it," I told him honestly.

"Well, how about coming with me? I was actually planning to go alone, but you've inspired me to take a date. If you do as well on the dance floor as you do on the soccer field, it'll be some evening."

"Thanks, that sounds great," I answered, but my mind was working fast. Should I refuse Jason on the chance that Rick would ask me?

That was my dream, but, of course, it didn't happen. Rick was silent on the subject.

When I told Gretchen and Amy about my date with Jason, they were floored.

"That's incredible," said Gretchen. "I guess your new look is really paying off."

"Aren't you excited?" asked Amy. "He's so cute."

"Sort of, but Jason's not really my type," I admitted.

"Who *is* your type, Jen?" Amy wanted to know.

"Well," I said hesitantly, "Rick Henley is awfully cute." Though he had been on my mind constantly since the first day of soccer, it was still hard for me to tell my friends about him.

"Uh, oh. I get the picture," said Gretchen gleefully.

I didn't feel so lonely once Gretchen and Amy knew about Rick. They joked about it a little, but they were really very sympathetic. And although they tried to be as helpful as they could be, when it came to attracting "special" boys, they were no more adept than I was. Amy and Roger were getting along great, but Roger, I knew, didn't have the nerve to show up at a dance. Gretchen was still watching the boys on the team from afar.

My parents' business was doing so well that they were only too glad to treat me to yet another new outfit, this one for the Harvest Moon Dance. After all, I had achieved startling results from my work.

There wasn't a moment to spare. Gretchen and Amy said they would come with me Saturday morning to shop. But when I told them I wanted to shop at a new punk boutique that had opened on Main Street, they were loud in their disapproval. We went, anyway, and I picked out a black, white, and brown leopard print jump suit and huge copper-colored earrings.

"This is a fall dance, not a Halloween party," Gretchen warned.

"Where's your spunk?" I challenged.

"Jenny, there is a difference between spunk and punk," she answered. "Next thing you know, you'll be dying your hair chartreuse and riding a motorcycle."

I got dressed for the dance that night, carefully applying the makeup that I had chosen with the help of the woman in the cosmetics shop. My short, wavy hair was styled with gel that gave it a wet look. Even my family was startled.

"Jenny, you look great," said Erin.

"Wow, look at Jenny," Roger said in disbelief as he leaned against the door to his room in sloppy sweats. "I still can't believe that Tremain is dating my sister!"

"Don't be such a chicken about going, Rog. You'd have a great time," I coaxed him.

"Not if I have to dress like that!" he answered.

"Who is this adult person?" my dad wanted to know.

"Where's my baby?" wailed Mom as she put her arm around me in a big hug. But there was a chuckle in her voice, and she went on to add, "Jen, you look absolutely fabulous."

I tried to act cool and sophisticated, in keeping with my appearance, but I was really nervous about going to my first dance. After all, I had never been in the gym for anything other than gym class or soccer team practice. And I was absolutely terrified of spending a whole evening with Jason Tremain. How would I ever think of enough things to say?

As it turned out, I needn't have worried. When Jason picked me up, he made no secret of his feelings about the way I looked. "Wow," he said as he took in my outfit. "You look fantastic." As we drove to school in his father's fancy red sports car, he proceeded to describe every soccer game he had ever played in. I sat back and listened. He didn't appear to want or expect anything but admiration from me.

The gym looked great, decorated with pumpkins and streamers, and the band sounded terrific. Jason loved to dance, and although I had been worried about it, he seemed not to notice. I was really uncomfortable about looking obviously inexperienced, so I started off slowly, doing my best to fake it. As I watched the kids around me, I started imitating what they were doing, and I think I did well enough to fool anyone.

Even though Roger had refused to come, quite a few of the boys from the team wandered in without dates and were eager to dance with me. It was great. I had never been the center of so much attention, except maybe when I broke my thumb playing basketball in sixth grade. Everyone kept telling me how great I looked, and Matt Schmidt said, "Wait until Stephanie sees you!"

It was a personal triumph to know I had achieved the glamorous look I had wanted. People were starting to think of me in the same way they thought of Stephanie. At least, *some* people were noticing the new me.

Chapter Six

As I danced with Jason and some of my soccer friends, I kept checking around for Rick. The gym was crowded with couples, but eventually I did spot him. Moving gracefully to the beat of the music, dressed in khaki pants and an olive cotton sweater, he looked gorgeous.

His partner was Stephanie, of course; I was prepared to see them together. What I wasn't prepared for was Stephanie's outfit. Her leopard print jump suit was just like mine!

She seemed to have discovered me just as I was looking at her, and our eyes met momentarily. Then she looked away, and I saw her say something in Rick's ear. He looked up as he danced and gave me a big grin.

Very funny, indeed, I thought to myself as I turned back to Jason. I threw myself into my dancing as if it were the only thing on my mind.

I was furious with myself. I had wanted to capture Stephanie's look, but I hadn't bargained for being her clone.

I wondered if Jason would say anything about the coincidence, but he never seemed to notice. He was just too busy being Jason.

When the band took a break, we sat down to have something to drink with a few other couples at one of the big tables decorated with rust-colored cloths and yellow and orange flowers. Jason saw Rick and Stephanie nearby and waved them over. As they approached, I could feel my stomach churning around.

"Hi, squirt," Rick greeted me.

"This is a squirt, Richard?" Stephanie wanted to know in a very superior voice.

"Hi. I'm Jenny Miller," I said. Looking her straight in the eye, I gave her my biggest smile.

"How do you do," she answered, without offering her own name. "Are you new around here?"

"I'd say she's very new," said Jason. "A newly arrived kid sister."

"We moved to North Hollow last year," I explained. "I like your outfit," I added, trying to be friendly. Stephanie only sniffed at this as she turned to talk to a small redheaded girl standing next to her.

"Looks like you're giving Stephanie a run for her money," Rick whispered in my ear. "And I think she's furious."

I was surprised by this confidence. I just managed to whisper back, "It's weird to be wearing the same outfit. I wish I could go home and change."

"Keep your chin, up, kid." he recommended, and I smiled at him weakly.

As we sat around the big table sipping our drinks, I knew things weren't working out exactly as I had hoped. I was powerless to make Rick notice me in a new light despite the all-out effort to change my image. I listened as he and Jason joked about something that had happened in English class, while Stephanie held court with all the most popular kids in school. A lot of kids who were gravitating around our table gave me friendly hellos, a few even stopped to talk about soccer. I was definitely sitting with the right crowd, not that I had ever thought about it before.

When the band came back from its break, Rick and Stephanie jumped up to dance. Jason was deep in conversation with Randy Hall, a boy from the team, and I was just as glad to sit and watch the dancers.

As I stared at the dance floor, I wanted desperately to know what drew Rick and Stephanie together. Rick, it seemed, really loved to dance, and so did Stephanie, but beyond that I was at a loss. Rick always seemed so easygoing and friendly. Stephanie was so cold and humorless.

Jason finished talking to Randy just as the band struck up one of my favorite old Beatle tunes, "I Want to Hold Your Hand."

"Want to dance?" Jason asked.

"I'd love to. This is one of my favorite songs."

"It is?"

"In fact, I love Beatle stuff in general," I went on to explain.

"They're OK, I guess," he said vaguely as we started to dance. My enthusiasm for the Beatles didn't seem to be contagious.

Rick and Stephanie were out there dancing next to us, and at that moment I wished more than anything I could dance with Rick, or at least talk to him. I was dying to know how he felt about the Beatles.

When the song ended, he and Stephanie were standing next to us.

"How about switching partners for the next one," Rick suggested. "I've got to get in at least one dance with squirt."

We all agreed, though I could see a frown on

Stephanie's face. It flattered me to know I was the cause of it.

I wanted the next dance to be slow, but no such luck. However, when the song began it had a good beat for dancing. It sounded oddly familiar, but I couldn't name it.

"Having a good time?" Rick asked as we moved to the rhythm.

I bobbed my head up and down and smiled. "Terrific."

"Great music," he went on. "Sounds like the band might be doing a whole sixties set."

"You think so? They just did a Beatles, but what's this?"

" 'Glad All Over' by the Dave Clark Five," he answered easily.

"How did you know that?" I asked, impressed.

"My older sister is a real sixties freak. My mother stored a carton of old records down in the basement, and my sister started playing them. They smelled incredibly dusty, but they sounded great."

"Really? What else is there?"

"Let me see," he began. "A lot of Beatles, of course, and Stones, and Jefferson Airplane, and the Lovin' Spoonful."

"Who's that?"

"A really nice group."

"I'd love to hear it sometime," I said shyly. "I love oldies."

"I'll see what I can do, squirt. I'm not sure if Beth took them to college with her."

We fell into our dancing again, and I looked over to Jason and Stephanie only to find Stephanie staring back at me. I turned away quickly. I wished that the music would go on forever. For the moment I had Rick, and I didn't want to give him back.

Not only was the music over too soon, but so was the dance. Rick didn't ask me to dance again during the course of the evening. I had to be content replaying every word he had said to me during our brief conversation, even while I danced with other people.

A lot of kids were going over to Jo-Jos afterward, and I gladly went with Jason. While I was with him, I thought, I was sure to see more of Rick.

But seeing Rick was not at all like being with Rick, and Stephanie kept him very well guarded. I'm not sure how she did it, but she managed to seat herself so that she and Rick were at the opposite end of the table from us. Jason and Rick were somehow close enough to yell jokes back and forth, but I was definitely in the backfield.

When he wasn't joking with Rick, Jason

spent time talking in my ear about where he wanted to go to college. Jason didn't expect answers to his questions or comments on his statements. In fact, he seemed to ignore them when they were offered. So rather than go to the trouble of trying to be witty, I just bobbed my head a lot as if I were listening. It was strange to think that he never noticed, but once I realized it, I let my mind wander to more interesting things like Rick and Stephanie.

Rick seemed like such a nice guy, such a special guy, and every time I spoke to him, I was even more drawn to his warm manner. Stephanie was unquestionably the queen of North Hollow, but she hadn't an ounce of warmth in her. Was that what people meant when they said opposites attract?

Around midnight as the crowd broke up, I was only too glad to leave. Watching Rick from across the table, yet not being able to talk to him, had been sheer torture.

On the way home Jason was silent as if he had talked himself out. It was a relief.

When he pulled into my driveway, he jumped out of the car and ran around to open my door. I was floored, to say the least. Then he walked me to the front door, and I said,

"Good night, Jason, thanks a lot for everything."

"It was fun, wasn't it," he said as he came up close, put his arms around me, and brought his face down to mine for a good night kiss.

It all happened so fast that I didn't have time to move away, but as his warm lips covered mine, I pulled back, confused and disinterested. "It was fun," I agreed. "But it's so late I think I'll go in now."

"I guess it is," he admitted, stepping back calmly. He seemed completely unaffected by my refusal to kiss him. "See you at practice, Jenny."

With that, I opened the front door, silently thanking my parents for having left it unlocked. No matter how calm Jason was acting, I was completely uncomfortable.

Flying up the stairs to my room, I felt tears of disappointment stream down my face. The evening had not turned out the way I had expected at all. I tossed my clothes and earrings into a corner and changed into my nightshirt. I furiously pulled my brush through my hair, brushing away the gel that had given it its glamorous style.

Why should I have to kiss a cute, but incredibly boring boy? And what about Rick? I was stunned to think about his taste in girl-friends. Stephanie was awful.

Suddenly I wanted desperately to be my old self again.

I didn't sleep very well, and the next morning when I finally got up, I pulled on an old ratty pair of jeans and a tattered T-shirt. My hair was sticking out in all directions despite a few brisk strokes with the brush, and I hardly cared.

Of course everybody in my family wanted to know about the dance.

"The band was great," I told them as we sat and ate the pancakes Dad had made for breakfast. "They played a set of sixties oldies that you would have liked, Roger."

"I'm sorry I didn't go," he said. "But I don't even know how to dance."

"Neither did I," I confessed. "And I was a little scared, but you just watch what the other kids are doing."

"What about Jason?" Erin asked.

"What about him?"

"Is he nice?"

"Well, if you really want to know, he's boring."

"Jenny, how can you say that?" asked Mom, shocked.

"Sorry, Mom, but he is," I explained

patiently. "He does too much talking and not enough listening."

"He is kind of conceited," acknowledged Roger. "The girls are always chasing him."

"Well, not this one," I promised. "One date with him was quite enough."

"Sounds like he bombed out in your book," said Dad.

"Did he kiss you?" Erin wanted to know.

"Erin, would you please mind your own business," I told her in my firmest voice. That was one subject I was not discussing with my family.

When breakfast was over, I went to my room to sulk. After all my hard work, I felt that I needed time to mourn for my smashed dreams.

My clothes for the dance were still in a heap where I had left them the night before, my hair dryer, gel, and makeup spread across my dresser, and I had no interest in picking any of them up.

Gazing in the mirror, I still didn't look like my old self. I was back in my comfortable old clothes, but gone was my practical, predictable ponytail. In its place was bizarre Cindy Lauper kind of hair sticking out all over my head.

I ran to the bathroom and stuck my head

under warm running water, toweled it off, and combed it quickly, glad to see it settle in place.

Gretchen and Amy arrived a little while later, eager for news of the dance.

"The whole thing was a disaster," I told them as we sat on a clear spot on the floor of my room. "Jason was just like I thought he would be, b-o-r-i-n-g, and he had the nerve to try to kiss me!"

"Jenny!" said Gretchen, much enthralled.

"It was gross, I can tell you. I listened to him rattle on about himself for four hours, and then he wanted to kiss me!"

I think they could tell I wasn't planning to discuss this very much. Neither of them pressed me on it, although I think they both would have liked to know more.

"Well, what about Rick?" Amy wanted to know.

"He was there, all right, with Stephanie, of course. And this is the most unbelievable part. She had on the same leopard print jump suit as mine."

Both my friends were startled. "What happened?" Gretchen asked. "Did she make it into a big deal?"

"No, she completely ignored it."

"Weren't you embarrassed?" asked Amy.

"I was mortified, and I was also furious with

myself for having bought it. I chose it because it was something I thought Stephanie might wear."

"Well, you were right," Amy said with a little laugh.

"Except I never knew what Stephanie was like before last night, and now that I know, I'm disgusted. I never want to wear that stupid jump suit again, or any of the other stuff I just bought that reminds me of her. And besides, I'm letting my hair grow back, too," I announced. Feeling myself crumble, I started to cry.

Amy and Gretchen sat on the floor and looked at me sympathetically.

"You sure sound miserable," said Amy.

"I am," I said. "And I was feeling so great yesterday. This just isn't fair."

"But what happened with Rick?" she asked. "You still haven't told us."

"It was horrible. I hardly got to talk to him all evening. He still thinks of me as Roger's kid sister, and it's probably going to be that way forever."

"I know how you feel," Gretchen said and sighed. "My brother in college has the cutest friends, and they just think of me as a kid, too. I can't stand it."

"Neither can I," I answered. "But there's

something else I can't stand, and that's Stephanie's personality. If Rick thinks she's so great, too bad for him. I'm not interested in a guy who's attracted to her type."

Chapter Seven

I felt much better after talking with my friends. Once I had sworn off Rick and his creepy girlfriend, we sat around in my room making Stephanie jokes. Then we decided to go to the movies.

A Hard Day's Night was playing at the Cinema Arts, and though we had all seen it about six times, we were always anxious to see it again. Roger and Matt came along, too, so Amy was flying high. Even Gretchen was starting to be more relaxed about talking to the boys, so we all had a good time.

Monday morning I went to school with a new attitude. In one way I felt that something was missing from my life because I had promised myself not to be on the lookout for Rick. On the other hand, it was an incredible relief not to worry about saying something brilliant at a moment's notice.

Although I had sworn off my newfound flashy style, I didn't want to be a slob anymore either, so I had to figure out a satisfactory compromise for myself. I ended up wearing a striped button-down shirt of Roger's over a turtleneck, clean jeans, and my black flats. I washed and styled my hair that morning, but I left off the gel as well as my eye makeup and big earrings. I felt more comfortable than I had in a long time.

I still had to change into sweats for soccer, but without the pressure of wanting to impress Rick, it wasn't painful at all. Of course, I was a little worried about what would happen when I saw Jason again, but as it turned out, he was friendly but cool. He didn't say a word about what had happened on our date. What a relief.

The weather had turned unpleasantly bitter, even for early November. It had been drizzling off and on since lunch, and Mr. Willens was in conflict about whether to hold practice outside or have the guys watch video tapes in the media room.

"We'll be playing on Monday unless it pours or snows," he told me as I waited for his decision. "But it's so nasty that I wonder if it might be better to go easy."

When the boys came in for practice, they

were eager to get on to the field. "How can I hold these guys back? I must be getting old. I've never been intimidated by a little bad weather before."

We warmed up in the gym and then did our jogs and sprints around the field. The team was all recovered from the flu season, and attendance was finally back to where it was supposed to be.

I joined them for the forward, backward, and sideways drills. I could see that the field was a lot more slippery in the center than it had been on the edges. Then the coach split them into two teams for a scrimmage, and since there were enough boys to make up the numbers, I stood on the sideline and watched.

Rick and Jason were working into unbeatable strikers while Roger and Randy Hall were dynamite halfbacks. Matt and Ted were great at sweeping across the backfield. Even Nicky, first-string goalie, seemed to have perfected his timing. The boys were riding high. But the ground was more slippery than usual, and after a few slides in the mud, the boys started horsing around. That's when disaster hit.

Roger, Jason, and Rick, messing with the ball, were trying to be the Harlem Globe Trotters of soccer. I could see the coach getting angrier and angrier, but as he blew his whistle to stop the play, Rick took a spill as his foot hit the ball, and he went down in the mud.

People fall in soccer all the time. A lot of times players go down willingly if it's the only way to make a shot. Then they pick themselves up and get on with the game.

We waited for Rick to pick himself up, but nothing happened. Jason, already well spattered from a fall or two of his own, yelled from across the field, "Henley, this is soccer, not mud wrestling." Still there was no response.

Finally Rick rolled over and tried to push himself up. But he slid back down again and let out a groan.

"Good grief," muttered the coach as he dashed across the field to Rick. "I had a feeling something like this was going to happen. Where does it hurt, Rick?"

"My wrist," he panted from the ground, the pain leaving him breathless.

It was horrible to watch Mr. Willens lead a mud-covered Rick to his car for a quick drive to the emergency room at North Hollow Hospital. Of course everyone wanted to go, but just Roger and Jason went, leaving the rest of us to pick up the equipment, wipe it and ourselves down, and shuffle on home.

Roger got back to the house about an hour after I did. "Rick broke his wrist," he told me.

"How is he?" I asked, feeling very sorry for him.

"From what he says, a lot better now that it's in a cast. The worst part is that he's finished with soccer for the season, and he's completely bummed out."

"I know the feeling well," I responded.

Rick came to practice the next day with his arm cast supported in a big red bandanna that was tied around his neck. The guys crowded around him to make jokes and sign his cast, while I stood back and watched.

The weather hadn't changed much since the day before, and Coach Willens decided to stay inside. So we did an extra long warm-up session in the gym while Rick watched from the bleachers looking very glum.

When warm-ups were over, we headed down to the AV room to look at tapes that the video club kids had made at a few of the scrimmages.

"Couldn't stay away, could you, Henley?" joked Randy Hall as we walked downstairs. "Talk about an addict. Are you planning to break the other arm?"

"Be serious, Hall," Rick answered. "The coach told me he was showing the tapes, and I didn't want to miss them."

We piled into the AV room, and I found myself sitting next to Rick. He hardly seemed to notice as we huddled around the television monitor.

It was fun to see the guys in action, even if the tapes were a little shaky. As the picture went blurry for the third time in a row, everyone groaned, and Coach Willens explained that the AV kids were still new at their jobs.

We watched about twenty minutes of play from three games while the coach pointed out good moves and bad moves. The boys teased each other back and forth about fouls. It took longer than twenty minutes because the coach kept stopping the tape to rerun a play, pointing out how an attack could have been made stronger, or a defense more effective.

"Strikers, you're not looking up from the ball. You're trying to be heroes, especially you, Tremain. Henley and Miller were out there waiting to help you," explained Mr. Willens in his tough tone. "And, backfield, let's get more of a sweep so we don't work our goalie so hard. Save his energies for the most dangerous attacks."

The coach gave as much attention to Rick's playing as he did to the other team members, finishing one of his critiques by saying, "You may be finished with soccer for this season, Henley, but you're not finished with soccer.

We're planning to get one more year out of you before you graduate." Everyone laughed.

I turned to see how Rick was taking this. His face had looked impassive before. Now, not only was he not smiling, but he looked downright miserable.

When the tapes were over and conversation filled the small room, I finally turned to Rick. I was sure he was feeling very down, and I wanted to say something encouraging.

"You look unhappy," I said, settling for understatement.

"I feel like such an idiot about this injury," he admitted.

"Why? It wasn't your fault."

"If I hadn't been so fast to show off, this might not have happened."

"Hey, you can't always know that," I assured him.

"Very wise, little one," he answered. Then he suddenly broke into a smile and ruffled my hair. It wasn't a romantic gesture, but it was a friendly one. I had already convinced myself that friendship was all there would ever be between us.

The Rick who had a broken wrist was a lot different from the Rick who played soccer. He showed up to watch all the practices, but he hardly ever smiled.

With Rick missing from the ranks, I was back in as the official substitute. But I felt bad about being out there because of his misfortune. And one day I told him so.

"Think nothing of it," he said, trying to be cheerful. "It's all in the way the ball bounces." He gave me one of his now rare smiles.

"Very funny," I answered quickly before I dashed out on the field to play.

Coach Willens was desperately trying to get Dave Rollins integrated into the front line before the final three games of our ten-game season. Jason, who hadn't been one hundred percent team oriented even when Rick was playing, seemed reluctant to accept Dave. Dave was only a sophomore—like me—but Willens thought that he had potential. But Jason tried to run the ball by himself, which had our usually unflappable coach clenching his fists and yelling at everyone.

During that practice I was playing on the second-string team. It was so much fun that I wanted more than ever to play on a team of my own.

Meanwhile, on the sidelines, Rick was not alone. Stephanie had figured that if Rick was benched, she could sit with him during practice. They looked content together, but I think Stephanie would have been a lot happier if she could have lured Rick away from the field. At one point, as I stepped behind the line to take a penalty kick, I heard him say, "Go ahead to Jo-Jos if you want, Steph. I'll meet you there after practice." I didn't hear her answer. She did hang around waiting for practice to end, though, but the look on her face seemed cooler than usual.

On Monday, at the first game North Hollow had since Rick's injury, the boys were very nervous. Easton High, with its 6—1 record, posed a serious threat to North Hollow, even though we were undefeated.

"Maybe their bus got lost," Nicky said. "And they'll have to forfeit the game." We were standing around waiting for them. But they arrived in plenty of time, and the game began on schedule.

Rick had come to the game as a spectator. As I sat at the table keeping the stats, I could hear him shouting encouragement to the team. The trouble was that they didn't seem to be listening.

I could tell by the way our team played that their minds weren't on the game. They were taking Rick's absence very hard. Easton sensed it, too, and in the first six minutes they scored their first goal against us. By halftime we were losing 2—0.

Coach Willens was furious, and at halftime he let them know it. "What's this, Christmas or something? Those goals were gifts from North Hollow. Let's not be so generous next time."

"He's right," said Rick sounding frustrated. "Come on, guys, we're so close to making the finals, we've got to get it together."

As the boys went back out to the field, Rick said to the coach, "I feel so bad that I can't be out there to help."

"Don't be so hard on yourself," he told him. "Let's not forget this is a team, not a one-man show. It's one thing to play your best and lose, but these clowns are just dragging their tails. That's what's so infuriating."

The boys started to perk up midway through the second half. Nicky made one stunning save at the goal. Roger and Dave did some beautiful assisting, and Jason was finally able to score a goal against Easton.

"Now you're cooking," the coach yelled to them. "Just a little more momentum, and you'll be making those points."

The coach assigned one of the third stringers to take the stat sheets from me because I needed a break badly. It wasn't that I minded keeping track of all the plays and penalties, but with an occasional break, I was able to concentrate better.

When I stood up from the table, I felt stiff. While I did some gentle muscle stretches, I let my mind wander.

The ground had dried up, and there was a brisk wind blowing. I was wearing jeans, a turtleneck, and a red-and-black-plaid flannel jacket. I had been warm enough when I was huddling over the table, but now that I was standing, I could feel the chill. I pulled my collar up around my neck and stuck my hands in my pockets.

"So what do you think? Are they going to get it together?" asked Rick as I stared out over the playing field.

"I really think they can," I told him. "I just don't know if they can do it for this game."

"It's driving me crazy not to be out there," he said with disgust.

"I bet," I agreed. "I'm impressed that you torture yourself by coming to the practices and games."

"I'm still part of the team, even if I can't play," he told me. "I'm not going to run out on the guys just because I can't have any fun with the ball."

I wanted desperately to be able to change the situation for him, or at least say something really helpful. Before I could say anything, however, Stephanie arrived. She was wearing a huge turquoise jacket with a purple scarf, and she looked great.

"How's it going, Rick?" she asked smoothly.

"Not too well," he admitted. "We're losing two to one."

They stood watching the game together for a few minutes. Once Rick shouted, "Hustle, you guys," but Stephanie just shook her head.

"Brother!" she said finally. "When is this thing going to be over? We're going nowhere in a hurry."

Stephanie had never bothered to acknowledge me since she had arrived, and I had stepped aside, feeling awkward. But her attitude of defeat was more than I could take.

"Don't be such a pessimist," I told her. "North Hollow can still get it together and make a comeback."

"Are you kidding?" she asked, irritated. Looking at me, I could tell she couldn't remember who I was.

"I'm Jenny Miller," I told her. "We met at the dance."

"Oh, yes," she said as if she had a vague, but unpleasant, memory of me.

We fell into silence, and as we stood there, our team performed some beautiful plays.

Then Roger passed the ball to Jason, who drove it into the corner of the goal. Rick and I went wild, cheering and yelling at the team to keep up the good work. Stephanie stood by, her expression unchanged.

The clock was running down. With about seven minutes left to be played, Rick and I watched every move out on the field. Once we shouted together, "Go for it, go for it."

Rick seemed to forget all about Stephanie as the excitement grew. Stephanie remained incredibly detached from the action. But I couldn't forget about her, and the more she frowned, the louder I cheered with Rick.

Chapter Eight

As it turned out, we tied the game with Easton 2–2, even with overtime. Although the boys were really down about not winning, Coach Willens had nothing but encouragement for them on Wednesday at practice. "You guys really perked up by the end of the game. It looks to me as if you're well on your way to recovery. We've just got to do it a little sooner next time," he added with a smile.

The morning had been gray and cold, but by the afternoon the sky had cleared. It had turned into a crisp fall day.

I did the warm-ups with the guys outside, and while we sprinted across the field, I noticed Rick hanging out on the sideline. At one point I noticed that Stephanie had joined him. A few laps later, she was gone.

The coach started to break the team into groups for cross-goal drills, but he seemed distracted. In the middle of assigning people to their groups, he suddenly turned to me.

"Jen, will you run down to the office and check on the bus for the game with Elwood next week. There was some question about whether we were entitled to it or not." He shook his head sadly. "Mrs. Waters ought to know by now."

"No problem," I told him, my face damp from wind sprints. As I headed off the field, Rick was suddenly by my side.

"Mind if I come along, squirt?" he asked.

"Be my guest, but please don't call me squirt."

He looked at me as if for the first time. Had I shocked him with my blunt request?

"I may be younger than you, but I don't like being called squirt," I explained.

"I'm sorry. I had no idea," he said. "Anyway, I tried to catch you before you got out on the field. I spoke to my sister last night on the phone, and she's got all those great albums with her at college. She says she'll bring them home next time she comes."

"Great," I told him. Actually I had put the records out of my mind so that I wouldn't be disappointed if he never mentioned them again.

"But she wasn't sure whether she'd be home his weekend or next," he explained.

"I'd love to hear them anytime," I answered.

After I told the coach that we had a bus for Tuesday's game, I joined the team for a practice scrimmage. As I raced up and down the field, I thought about my conversation with Rick. Had I been too cool in my response to his offer? Did he understand that not only was I anxious to hear his records, but I was also eager to spend time with him?

Although I had sworn off trying to "attract" Rick, there was no doubt in my mind that I would be drawn to him always. But as desperately as I wanted him to notice me, I also didn't want to make a fool of myself.

I felt a lot more mature than I had a few weeks before. I realized that I had been wrong to think that looking a certain way would make Rick see me in a different way. There was more to it than that.

I liked Rick because, in addition to his good looks, he was also friendly, relaxed, cheerful, and energetic. If he was going to like me, it was going to have to be because I was me, Jenny Miller. If he was attracted to a different kind of person, I would just have to learn to live with it.

Once again I resolved to put him out of my

mind. It turned out to be easier than I had expected because so much started to happen at once.

At four-thirty practice broke up, and Coach Willens came up and put his arm around my shoulder. "Jenny, stop in my office before you go, will you?" I nodded, and he walked away.

It was an uncharacteristic request made in an uncharacteristic way, and I was completely mystified. I put away the equipment quickly and headed into his office.

He was sitting at his desk, wearing his reading glasses and looking over some papers. "Close the door, will you?" he asked me in his no-nonsense voice.

"Did something terrible happen?" I asked, trying to laugh away my apprehension.

"No, not really," he told me quickly. "Actually, it's something wonderful for you. It's just not so great for me. I guess I'd better explain," he added, seeing my confused expression. "Earlier today I was talking with a friend who coaches the girls' traveling soccer team over in Highland Park. She's having a nasty season with injuries and illnesses. Anyway, she's inviting a select group of out-of-town girls to try out day after tomorrow for the slots in the team. Even though Highland is a few miles away, and transportation could be a factor, I told her I had just the girl for her."

"Me?" I asked, astonished.

"Absolutely, Miss Miller," he said. "I've been watching you all season, and it's a crying shame that you haven't got a team to play on. It's too bad that North Hollow hasn't done what some other towns have done, organized independent teams and formed an independent league. But since North Hollow hasn't, there's no reason why you shouldn't play over there."

"Coach Willens, I can't believe this. It seems too good to be true."

"Well, there are a few hurdles," he reminded me. "First, you do have to try out—not that I imagine that that will be any problem. And second, the practices are Monday, Wednesday, Friday. The games are mostly on Saturday or Sunday, and you'll have to get yourself back and forth to Highland Park. That's about ten miles from here."

"Maybe my parents can drive me over."

"And if you make the team, there's a membership fee to cover expenses, though most of the traveling is done through the good graces of volunteer parents."

"I'll baby-sit five nights a week to raise the money." I laughed.

"Finally, the season is well underway. If it works out, it'll give you a good edge for making their team next year. Here's Coach Mayall's home number," he said, smiling as he handed me a piece of yellow lined paper from the pad on his desk. "She's expecting to hear from you tonight."

"I just can't believe it," I said again as I folded the paper and clutched it in my hand. "But isn't their season almost over?"

"You would think so," he agreed. "But the travel teams go a little later because they only have games on weekends. Is that a problem? You look confused."

"It's only that I won't be here all the time for the North Hollow varsity if I play in Highland Park."

"That's definitely a minus," Coach Willens agreed. "But with two games left, I'm sure the boys can get the work done themselves. Not that we won't miss you, because we really will. But how could anyone deny you the chance to play soccer? You've given us a lot, and it's our turn to give you something in return."

I ran home flying high and told Roger the great news. But he was less than thrilled. "What about the North Hollow varsity?" he asked. I assured him that they would survive, trying to repeat exactly what the coach had said to me.

"Coach is sure you guys are going to be OK," I told him.

"I know, but I can't help it if I'm a little nervous," Roger said glumly.

I called Coach Mayall, who sounded really friendly on the phone. She spoke with a mild British accent, which made me even more excited. Soccer was invented in England, and it had been popular there for a long time, so I thought maybe she would have a real love and knowledge of the game. Sometimes well-meaning, inexperienced parents end up coaching. For a serious player it can be a real letdown.

Tryouts were going to be held at the Highland Park town field on Friday afternoon, and there were eight other girls trying out for the three spaces.

At dinner that night I told the rest of my family about the Highland Park tryouts.

"That's really exciting," my dad said. "Are you going to let Roger give you some pointers beforehand?"

"I don't think Roger wants me to make it," I said quietly.

"Well, it means that we'll be without a manager again," Roger complained.

"Just for next week. The season's over then," I reminded him.

"Roger, can we have a little enthusiasm for your sister?" requested Mom, but he just grunted. "Jenny, your dad and I will be glad to get you back and forth to Highland," she assured me. "And maybe your brother will even pitch in, right?" Roger shook his head, but he didn't say a word.

When dinner was over and the kitchen cleaned up, I sat down at the counter and called my friends on the phone. The kitchen was empty. Roger and Erin were upstairs doing their homework, and my parents were in the den looking over a real estate offer.

Gretchen's line was busy, so I automatically dialed Amy. Amy is one of those lucky people who has her own phone in her room. When she picked it up, I said, "It's Jenny, and I have such great news." I then proceeded to tell her about the Highland soccer tryouts.

"I know," she told me when I was done. "I just spoke to Roger, and he's very freaked out."

"You know," I complained, "what my brother needs is a heavy dose of self-confidence."

"Don't we all," said Amy.

"Well, while we're on the subject of self-confidence, I did the most gutsy thing today," I told her, remembering the rest of my afternoon. "I told Rick Henley to stop calling me squirt. It's been driving me up a wall lately."

"And what happened?"

"It was unbelievable. First he apologized, and then he told me he wanted to play some sixties albums for me."

"That's great!" Amy said excitedly.

"He didn't name a definite time, and it wasn't the most romantic-sounding invitation," I said.

"Are you complaining?" she asked.

"Nope," I said. "And besides, I'm not even interested in Rick Henley anymore," I added for good measure.

"Oh, right," said Amy sarcastically. We chatted for a while and then hung up.

By the time I got to practice the next day, practically every member of the team had stopped me in the hall, the lunchroom, or the library to either complain or congratulate me on the Highland Park team.

"Hey, wait a minute, I haven't even made it yet," I reminded Matt when he gave me his reluctant good wishes.

"Jenny, honestly, how could you not!"

During our scrimmage that afternoon, I suddenly realized that everyone was going out of his way to pass me the ball. The coach had put me on the front line, and I found it suspiciously easy to score.

"Come on, you guys," I said after my second pushover goal. "This is fun, but it's not much of a challenge."

"Hey," said Matt, "we want to make sure you get enough practice so you can show those people in Highland just how serious we are here in North Hollow."

The nicest thing by far was what Rick had to say. "Roger told me that you're trying out for the travel team in Highland Park, Jenny. I'd wish you good luck, but I'm sure you'll do just fine. And don't worry about the manager job here. I've already told the coach I'll be glad to fill in," he finished.

"Thanks a lot, Rick, but what about your wrist?"

"It's doing just fine, and whenever I can't handle something, I'll just draft someone from the third string. I'm planning to do the statistics myself."

"It's not that hard," I told him. "Mostly a matter of concentration. But even without a broken wrist, I usually need somebody to cover for part of the second half."

"Hey, no problem. Just do well tomorrow."

Rick sounded more cheerful than he had

since his accident. It was nice to see him back to his old self. Was he glad that I was leaving the team, or just happy for my good fortune?

I had no time to worry about Rick because I was a little nervous about the tryouts. My dad drove me over to the Highland Park fields, and Roger and Erin came along. I had only been there once or twice, so I felt like a real outsider. That didn't help my already strung-out nerves.

It was easy to recognize Coach Mayall. She was a big, tall woman in her early forties with short, sandy-colored, curly hair. She was wearing a red wool jacket that said "Highland Park Soccer Coach" across the back.

I didn't know any of the eight other girls who were trying out, although some of them seemed to know the girls on the Highland team.

Coach Mayall gave each of us a number to pin to our shirts and introduced the nine of us to her team. She told us each girl's position and acknowledged that it was going to be difficult for us to remember who everyone was out on the field. She then assigned us to various positions. After twenty minutes we would switch to the front line or backfield, so we could have a chance to play in each.

Then Coach Mayall explained that we would

be watched and rated by her, as well as her assistant coach, Mr. Morrow, and Mr. Elkin, the boys' coach from Highland Park High.

As the scrimmage got underway, I suddenly felt I was at a great disadvantage. With the boys' team I had gotten to know what to expect from each guy. Now, just when I wanted to do my best, I wished I knew the playing habits of these girls.

I could have played a lot worse. Once or twice I found that I had broken through the backfield with surprising ease. I made a long, clean pass to one of the other girls who was trying out; she was able to drive it into the cage.

Of course I did have a pang of envy when she scored the point, but I reminded myself that we were out there to play as a team.

When the playing time was over and we had each taken a turn in the front line and back-field, we came off the field, laughing and sweating. My team lost 4—2. I had scored one goal, and the girl I'd passed to, Ruth, had scored the other. I wondered if the girls on the other team would automatically be chosen, though one girl seemed to have done all of the good playing.

Ruth and I tried to joke with each other while we sipped the orange juice that had been handed to us. I could see that the judges were already conferring on the edge of the field.

My dad, Roger, and Erin waved and gave me the thumbs-up sign, which made me laugh, but they stayed where they were as I hung out with the soccer players. It was awkward to be a stranger, but Ruth and I seemed to be able to talk easily. She was a tall, muscular girl with a really pretty face and dark brown hair that came to her shoulders.

"I like the way you play soccer," I told her honestly.

"Thanks, I like the way you play, too," she said. "But isn't it weird when you don't know what anybody can do? You're not sure who to look for."

"You can say that again," I agreed.

We joked for a bit while we awaited the decision, and I wondered if Ruth could tell how anxious I was. Was she as nervous as I was?

The tension wasn't going to last much longer. Within a few minutes Coach Mayall came over to the crowd of new and old players.

"May I have your attention, please?" she asked in her neat British accent. "I want to thank all of you for coming out to play with us today. You all did admirably. Unfortunately, we can only take three of you right now, and those who have been selected are the following: Ruth Chasen, Janet Rosenbaum, and Jenny Miller. Congratulations, girls."

The team cheered. Ruth and I joined hands and jumped up and down as if we were old friends.

Chapter Nine

Dad and Erin were as thrilled as I was, and even Roger was properly enthusiastic about my making the team. I couldn't wait to tell my mom and my friends.

When we got back to the house, Mom gave me a big hug. "Jenny, you must be so excited. I'm so happy for you."

I ran to the phone to call Amy and Gretchen while Roger set the table for dinner. I even called Coach Willens who gave me his heartiest congratulations. But I realized I didn't have the nerve to call the person I really wanted to tell—Rick Henley. I thought I had done such a good job of ridding myself of my romantic notions about him, but I was still intimidated by the idea of calling him.

I had a lot of reading to do for English, so I put Rick firmly out of my mind. I went upstairs after dinner and opened my book. At quarter to ten, as I was fighting to stay awake through *Moby Dick*, the phone rang.

"Jenny, it's for you," shrieked Erin from downstairs. "It's Rick Henley, and I told him you made the team. I hope you don't mind."

"I'll take it up here," I called back, wondering what I had done to deserve being so humiliated by my little sister.

Going into my parents' bedroom, I sat down on the bed and picked up the phone.

"Hello," I said, trying hard to sound relaxed.

"Congratulations," said Rick warmly. It was nice to hear his voice. "I guess it went OK in Highland. Were you the runaway star?"

"Try again," I said, laughing. "I held my own, and I made it. I've got a lot of work to do before I'm a great player."

"It'll come," he assured me.

"I know, but I wish it would come fast, like tomorrow."

"Don't we all," he acknowledged. "Anytime I can give you pointers, let me know," he offered without a hint of superiority. "Sometimes it's a lot easier to help somebody than it is to do something yourself."

"Thanks, I may just take you up on that. Roger used to be my best coach, but he's still angry about my deserting the team."

"What? I'll have to talk some sense into that

turkey. Is he around? Put him on," Rick demanded.

"You must be joking," I said.

"I've never been more serious."

"Hold on. I'll find him." Putting the phone down, I raced out of my parents' room and down the hall to Roger's room. "Rick wants to talk to you," I told him as I stood at the door to his room. He was lying on his bed reading *Soccer World*.

"Oh, sure," he mumbled as he untangled his long legs from the bed. Then he disappeared down the hall and into my parents' bedroom.

I hung around outside the room, dying to know what Rick was going to say to my brother. I could only get a vague idea of the conversation from Roger's end. At first there was silence, and then Roger answered, "You realize, Henley, that we'll be back to square one without Jen." Again there was a pause while Rick must have given his rebuttal in my defense.

"Uh-huh, uh-huh," responded Roger. "Well, if you really want the job, who am I to complain?"

When Roger hung up, he went back to his room without saying a word to me about his conversation with Rick. I could only guess

what Rick had said. Although I really appreci-
ated his efforts, I couldn't understand why he
would bother.

The next day, Saturday, I got up early to run
with Dad and Roger. But Roger didn't answer
my knock on his bedroom door, so we went
without him.

"I'm so excited about making the soccer
team," I told my dad as we did our muscle
stretches on the back patio, "but Roger is being
a real pain." The air was chilly, and I was anxious to start running so I'd warm up.

"He *is* being a little sensitive," Dad agreed.
"But you know how crazy he is about the
team."

"But he's acting like I committed a crime."

"That's not like him," Dad agreed. "Hang in
there, Jenny, and try not to let him get you
down. I wonder what's upsetting him more,
losing his team manager, or losing his sister."

"Really, Dad. That's completely dumb."

"No, it's not," he assured me as we took off
down the street at a slow pace. "You may not
have realized it, and maybe he hasn't either,
but Roger is definitely affected by the changes
in his kid sister. Now that the boys on the
team have realized that you're not just one of

them, but one terrific girl, Roger is absolutely confused."

"Daddy, that's not true," I said, and I almost lost the rhythm of my stride.

"Of course it is, Jen, and that's as it should be. Your poor brother just doesn't know how to deal with this. He's bouncing back and forth between being proud and being jealous."

"Well, it's sure a pain," I repeated.

"Hang in there, and I predict he'll get himself together soon. He's just got to get things in perspective."

When we finished our run and got back to the house, Roger was sitting in the kitchen with Mom and Erin. Roger was reading through the sports pages, Mom was reading through the real estate section, and Erin was cracking eggs into a bowl, discarding the shells all over the kitchen counter.

"We're having french toast for breakfast," she told Dad and me.

"What time do you have to be in Highland Park?" Mom asked. "I'll be glad to give you a lift."

"Twelve-thirty. Is that OK?"

"Sounds fine."

"Have a big breakfast and a light lunch, and you'll do a lot better," advised Roger.

"Hey, thanks, Rog." I was pleased and surprised by his show of concern.

"Good thing I'm making a nutritious breakfast," put in Erin.

"Absolutely," agreed Dad, but it was quickly followed by a surprised, "Good heavens, Erin, just how many people are you planning to feed? It looks like you've gone through a dozen eggs."

"I have," she said proudly. "You always say how much you like my french toast, so I wanted to make sure we had enough."

There was no way I would have been able to eat a big lunch later that morning. By eleven-thirty I was feeling too nervous to seriously consider much more than plain yogurt and fruit. After all, I was about to practice with a team of girls who all knew one another. My skills were rusty, and I wanted to do my best.

When my mom drove me over, I must have been unusually quiet.

"Nervous, Jen?" she asked.

"Yes," I admitted. "It's definitely scary to walk into the middle of a team that has been playing together. I have no idea how they'll feel about me. It could be awful."

"Be brave," she told me. "You can never know how things will turn out, and sometimes you find that you've worried for nothing." I nodded to let her know that I'd do my best. "Now, Jen," she went on, "somebody will pick you up, but Saturdays can be really hectic at the office. If we're a little late, don't think we've forgotten you."

We had pulled into the parking lot next to the playing field, and she leaned over and gave me a kiss on the cheek. "Have a great time," she told me.

As it turned out, my mother had been right in her prediction. Ruth and I arrived at the field at just the same time, so I didn't have to walk into the crowd alone. Janet, the other new girl, was already there when we arrived. The Highland girls were glad to have us. By the end of practice, I felt as if I still wasn't playing my best, but at least I felt welcome.

I had been so anxious to do well that I pushed myself really hard during practice. I came off the field at the end of it sweaty and exhausted from having put myself under such pressure.

I waved goodbye to the girls as they streamed off in all directions.

"Do you need a ride, Jenny?" asked Coach Mayall, concerned that I was the last of her team still on the field.

As I was assuring her that I expected to be

picked up a little late, I saw our green Dodge at the corner light.

"My ride's here now," I said. "See you tomorrow."

"Yes, indeed," she agreed. "And you're doing just beautifully."

I ran to the end of the parking lot to save Mom or Dad the trouble of having to circle around. As I opened the back door, I was startled to discover that it was Roger who was driving, and he wasn't alone. I was sitting behind Rick. I pulled the door shut and buckled my seat belt.

"Look who I found down at Sanderson's. The one-man Jenny Miller Fan Club," Roger said.

I was overheated, streaked with sweat and dirt—and very embarrassed. But Rick was quick to smooth over the situation. "Hey, Roger, all I said was that it wasn't fair for your sister to miss the chance to play soccer because of us." He had turned sideways so he could look at both of us.

"I know, I know," conceded Roger. "I've been getting that message from a lot of people, and, Jen, I'm sorry I've been so lousy about it. Of course it's a lot easier to take since Henley promised he'd be manager." He said this staring straight ahead as if it were too embarrassing to look me in the eye. I knew how hard it was for Roger to admit he was wrong about something.

"So anyway, Jen," Roger said changing the subject as he drove away, "Rick and I decided we just can't wait to get the Regional Soccer Newsletter to find out how the other varsity teams are doing. We're going to the Highland Sports Shop to see if they have it. It's not much out of the way. Do you mind?"

"No, except if I don't get some food in me soon, I'm going to die of starvation." I said it lightly, but I was really hungry.

"I think we could manage to find you something to eat in Highland, Ms. Miller," said Rick. "In fact, the sports shop happens to be conveniently located next to a great diner, the Shipwreck."

Roger parked the car at a meter on Main Street and rushed into the sports shop, emerging a few seconds later with a grin on his face, clutching the newest issue of the Soccer Newsletter.

"You've got to hustle if you want to get what you want," he announced happily.

"But, Roger, don't you have a subscription to that?"

"Yes, but I won't get the new issue until at least Wednesday."

"It's hard to imagine that the season is almost over—we're done next week," put in Rick.

The three of us climbed the steps of the diner, which was decorated with wooden steering wheels from boats as well as other nautical paraphernalia.

I ordered a cheeseburger, fries, and a vanilla milk shake, while Rick ordered a chocolate shake. Roger didn't order.

"How could I eat at a time like this?" he asked, almost annoyed at my insensitivity. "I've got a lot of reading to do."

Roger immersed himself in the statistics on high-school soccer teams around the state. He was anxious to know whether North Hollow had a chance to make it into the national playoffs, and then the championship games in Europe.

"And this is what's known as an obsession, folks," Rick told me in his Howard Cosell voice, holding his hand up to his mouth as if it were a microphone. Roger, ignoring his comments, kept studying the columns of numbers.

"So how was practice?" Rick asked when we realized that Roger had retreated into his own world.

"It was great," I told him. "But I could be doing a lot better, and that's really frustrating."

"Don't worry," he assured me. "Give yourself some time. How's the coach?"

"She seems good, but I think she's more than a little overwhelmed by taking on three new people so close to the end of the season. With one practice before a game, it's hard to know where to put us. How can she possibly know what we can do?"

He shook his head.

"I don't know either," I told him. "But tomorrow's game isn't supposed to be too competitive. The Tailor team is pretty weak, from what everybody says."

"What time is the game tomorrow? Maybe I'll come."

"One-thirty, but you can't! I'll be so embarrassed."

"Why?"

"Because I'm still so awful."

"I don't believe that for a second," he said with a smile.

The waitress put my shake and burger down in front of me, and as I looked at it I suddenly lost my appetite. Exhaustion had finally set in, and I was just too tired to eat.

Rick must have understood the expression on my face because after a few seconds of silence, he said, "Take a bite, and you'll feel a lot better."

"It's so weird. All of a sudden, I'm not hungry."

"I know the feeling well," he said. "But if you eat a little something, usually it comes back. And you look like you could use a little food."

"Gee, thanks."

"I didn't mean to say you look bad," he explained. "But when you exhaust yourself playing, you really do need something to eat."

I had a sip of my shake, and it tasted so good, I ended up devouring it as well as the burger and fries.

"You were right," I told Rick.

When we were both finished, we had to rouse Roger from his newsletter.

"You've been delightful company, Roger old boy," joked Rick. "We'll have to do it again sometime soon." But Roger just mumbled, immune to Rick's humor.

"You know, North Hollow's really got a chance to make it into the nationals if we can just win the rest of our games," he told us as we got up from the table.

But just before we reached the door, it opened toward us, and we stood back as Jason Tremain and Stephanie Danworth came in, chatting together happily. At least, they seemed really happy until they discovered the three of us standing in the diner.

"Oh, hi, guys," said Jason. He sounded very uneasy. "Stephanie has been telling me about the shakes in this place, and I thought I should give one a try."

"They're great," agreed Rick. "Especially the chocolate." His casual tone surprised me. "Well, see you around," he told them and went out the door. Roger and I followed him.

"You know, if we win our last two games, we'll be in really good shape for the state and the nationals," Roger repeated as if he had missed the significance of what had just happened. But Rick, despite his carefree tone, seemed suddenly withdrawn, as if he were in shock. I was pretty shocked myself.

"Well, that was weird," said Rick, as if he were thinking out loud. I had to agree with him.

"You must have been very surprised," I said.

"Yes and no," he answered, but he offered me no further explanation.

We all climbed into the car and Roger started the motor. He began to regale us with the local league scores and standings as we headed back to North Hollow.

There was no way Rick and I could get a word in edgewise. It was probably just as well.

My friendship with Rick was based on soccer, and I was afraid I wouldn't know what to say if I had to talk about anything else. When it came to talking about Stephanie and Jason, I was definitely out of my league.

As we passed the Welcome to North Hollow sign, Roger broke off his monologue long enough to invite Rick to our house.

"Henley, want to hang out at our place, or do you want me to drop you home?"

I felt myself tense up as I waited for his answer. I wanted him to come over, but I knew I would be a nervous wreck if he did.

"Thanks, Rog," he answered. "I'd love to, but I promised to help my dad with some stuff at home. We're stripping the wallpaper in the dining room."

"How can you manage it with your arm in a cast?" I asked.

"I'm going to scrape with my good arm. It might be fun, for a while."

We dropped Rick at his Tudor-style house, only a few blocks away from our house. When the front door closed and Rick was out of sight, I felt a wave of disappointment that our time together was over.

"Henley is some guy," said Roger as we drove home. "I really like him."

"Me, too," I mumbled.

"It's no wonder all the girls are crazy about him."

"Like who?" I asked, wondering if my feelings showed.

"Like Amy," he said with a heartfelt sigh.

"Amy! Really, Roger, Amy is crazy about *you*."

"*Yeah?* How do you know?" he challenged.

"She told me, that's how. In fact, both Amy and Gretchen think you're really cute, and so do a lot of other girls."

"Oh, yeah? Amy really likes me?" His voice perked up.

"Absolutely."

"You know," he said, "I like Amy a lot, and we're always talking on the phone, but I'm not like Henley. And I keep wondering if she likes him better."

"Well, she doesn't," I said flatly. "You're the one she talks about all the time. I think you ought to do more things together. I hope this doesn't make you mad, but honestly, Roger, you're letting soccer take over your life."

"I'm not mad, but I don't think you're right."

"OK, forget I said it," I told him. "But if I were Amy, I'd want to talk about something else sometimes, too. Why don't you ask her out to a movie or something?"

We drove the rest of the way home in silence. I hoped that Roger was thinking about what I had just said.

On Sunday my first game with my new team went OK. It wasn't great, just OK. My whole family came to see me play, and I almost wished they hadn't.

We won the game 3–2, but with Tailor's record we should have done a lot better. We had some distance to go before we played our very best.

The most difficult part was in the middle of the second half. I looked up and saw Rick standing next to Roger. I think maybe I did a little better because he was there, but it still wasn't good enough.

When the game was over, Coach Mayall called us together for a few words of congratulations and encouragement. "You girls are just warming up," she told us. "Now go home and rest, and I'll see you all tomorrow."

After saying goodbye to everyone, I headed for the parking lot with my family and Rick.

"I caught the last twenty minutes of the game," Rick told me. "You looked as if you were really getting it together."

"Thanks. I felt things start to come together toward the end. I can hardly wait to get back to practice tomorrow. Oops!" I said quickly. "I'm sure that's hard for you to take right now."

"Hey, no problem," he assured me. "Besides, breaking my wrist gave me the chance to be the team manager."

"Being manager was a lot of fun, and I miss it in a way. Listen to me, I've been gone a few days and already I'm feeling nostalgic." We both laughed.

"What's wrong with that? Besides, that's one of the things I wanted to talk to you about," Rick said.

My family was already in the car.

"Nostalgia?" I asked, signaling to them that I'd be right along.

He nodded. "Remember the old records I was telling you about? Well, my sister got home last night with a bunch of them, and I wondered if you'd like to come over for a little while before dinner today to hear them."

"That sounds like fun," I answered, and then I stopped myself, remembering that I had just played a vigorous hour and a half of soccer. "But I'm too disgusting to go anywhere." I was covered with dirt, sweat, and grass stains, and I was wearing my red and white Highland Park uniform complete with shin guards, knee pads, and cleated shoes.

"No problem," Rick said. "I've got to go by

the hardware store, and I'll pick you up at your house when I'm done."

"You've got a deal," I told him, slapping five to his outstretched hand. Then I turned and floated to my family's car.

Chapter Ten

"It's great to see you playing soccer again," my mom said as we headed home in our car.

"You did great," complimented Roger. "Was I ever surprised to see Henley."

"He had to go to a hardware store in Highland Park that's open on Sundays," I explained, secretly wondering if he really had come to see me.

"Hey, Dad, can we stop at McDonald's?" Erin asked as we neared the outskirts of North Hollow.

"I don't see why not," Dad answered cheerfully. "Anybody have any pressing engagements?"

"Could you drop me off at the house first?" I asked, anxious to avoid revealing my reasons. Erin can be a terrible tease, and I wasn't in the mood to deal with her.

Erin gave me a dirty look.

"Actually, I have to get home, too," chimed in my mother. "I'm expecting a call."

"Oh, Mom," groaned Erin.

"Don't worry," replied Dad. "We'll drop them off at the house and go back."

When we got home, I rushed upstairs for a quick shower. Under the stream of water, I tried to decide what to wear. No matter how hard I tried to convince myself otherwise, I knew that I still wanted to attract Rick.

There wasn't a lot of time to stew over my options. I ended up dressing very casually, and not all that differently from my old sloppy self. But I had learned to make small changes. I wouldn't have thought they would have made a big difference, but when I looked in the mirror, I realized that they did.

I had put on Roger's big blue-striped sweater, one that he never wore, and neat jeans. I styled my hair quickly with the blow dryer; I was happy that it was so short. Then I put on a pair of bright blue plastic earrings that I had seen in the drugstore and hadn't been able to resist.

When I was finished, I checked myself over in the mirror. I definitely liked what I saw. I looked feminine and pretty, and not over-dressed. Suddenly I felt good about myself and my life, and no matter what happened—or didn't happen—with Rick and me, I was glad to be going to listen to oldies with him.

Rick rang the bell thirty minutes later. I ran down the steps just as my mother got to the door.

"I'm going over to Rick's to listen to records," I told her as I grabbed my jacket and bag and ran out the front door.

As we walked down the front walk to get into Rick's family's car, the rest of *my* family pulled up. I gave them a quick wave and jumped into the front seat next to Rick.

"If Erin knows where we're going, she'll want to tag along," I confessed.

"Well, not to be mean or anything, she's not invited," he said. "And I'll be glad to tell her as gently as I can."

"What's the matter? Don't you like kid sisters?" I teased.

"Yes, but there's a time and a place for everyone," he said. "And this time, right now, is for us."

I loved the way he said that. My stomach did a definite flip-flop. I wasn't sure what to say back, so I ended up saying nothing.

"How's the wallpaper removal?" I asked instead.

"It's great. My sister got home and took over

for me. It's a lot easier for her with both arms working."

"What about driving?" I asked, suddenly concerned. Rick was no longer wearing his sling, and he had both hands on the wheel.

"It's fine, believe me," he said, "or I wouldn't be out fooling around like this."

He pulled into his driveway, and I followed him into the house through the garage. "We can avoid the mess in the dining room this way," he explained. He was wrong. When we walked into the kitchen, there were buckets and plastic bags filled with old wallpaper all over the floor.

Rick's father and his sister Nancy were sitting at the kitchen table dressed in old jeans and work shirts. Rick's dad, with his short gray hair, looked a lot older than my father. When he smiled, he looked a lot like Rick.

"Glad to see you've brought reinforcements," said Mr. Henley, giving me a friendly wink.

"You look just about right for this job," added Nancy, rolling her eyes. "But you've got to get into work clothes."

"In case you don't remember, you guys, Jenny came to hear some of Mom's old records."

"Oh, right. The ones you made me drag home from school," said Nancy.

"Whoops," I said. I didn't know whether she was teasing or not.

"She's putting you on," Rick said quickly. "She brought them home so I could tape them. In fact, maybe I'll give you the tapes to take back, Nance, so we don't have to worry about the records getting destroyed."

"Well, maybe," she said. "I'll have to think about that."

"But I'm not going to waste time talking to you. You've got too much work left," said Rick. Then he added, "Jenny, I'm the world's best egg cream maker. Would you like me to make you one?"

"I hate to sound stupid, but I don't even know what it is," I confessed.

"Not many people do. You have to be from Brooklyn, like the Henleys. We lived there until I was twelve. Do you like chocolate and soda?"

"Yes."

"Then you'll like an egg cream. It's a drink."

"What about the egg part? Is it raw?"

"Funny thing about egg creams. When they wrote the recipe, someone forgot the egg."

"Sounds weird," I said.

I stood by the counter as Rick mixed seltzer,

milk, and chocolate syrup in two tall glasses using what he assured me were scientific proportions. Then he stirred both glasses with a long spoon.

"Hmm, delicious," I told him as I took a sip from my glass.

"Bring it in the den, and I'll put on some records."

"Put the stereo on loud so we can hear it," suggested Nancy as we went out.

Rick set up the cassette deck to tape the music as the record played. We sat down on a brown corduroy couch to listen to Peter, Paul, and Mary, one of Rick's favorite groups from the sixties. Although their name was familiar, I had never heard them before, and I liked their clean, strong folk sound.

As we listened, the phone rang. In a few seconds Nancy was standing at the doorway to the den wearing a white painter's cap and holding a scraper. "Rick, it's for you," she said.

"I love the song after this," he told me as he turned down the stereo slightly and picked up the phone on the desk.

"Hello?" he said, his voice bright. "What's up?" he asked. "No, don't be silly. I'm not mad," he assured the caller, but it was easy to tell from the sudden change in his voice that something was bothering him. "But I already told her that I'm not coming. Really. OK. Bye."

Rick hung up the phone and took a deep breath. "That was Jason," he told me.

"You sound upset," I said hesitantly. Did he care if I noticed?

"Well, I guess I am," he admitted. "I'll tell you about it sometime, but I don't think I can talk about it right now."

He sounded really distressed, and although I could only imagine that something bad had happened with Stephanie, I couldn't imagine the details.

We went back to listening to Peter, Paul, and Mary. Rick seemed to be able to put the phone call out of his mind, returning to his fun, cheerful self. But I couldn't help trying to guess what had happened. It seemed obvious that Jason and Stephanie were hanging out together and Rick was very hurt.

But whatever it was, Rick wasn't letting it interfere with our time together. We listened to five or six more albums, Buddy Holly with the Crickets, the Everly Brothers, and the Dave Clark 5, among them. We had a great time, or at least I did. I think Rick did, too. Much too soon it was time for me to go home for dinner.

Since Rick definitely did not want to discuss

Stephanie and Jason, I tried to call Gretchen and Amy when I got home. Here was something I knew they could get into. But they were both away for the weekend, Amy at a swim meet upstate, Gretchen at her grandmother's in New York City. Neither of them were home yet. I called several more times, but by eleven o'clock I gave up and went to bed.

The next day at school they both seemed a little sleepy eyed as we sat in the commons talking about an English assignment that we had just gotten. Tired as they seemed, they were certainly awake enough to notice Stephanie and Jason as they strolled in front of us, deep in conversation.

"Will you look at that," Gretchen whispered to us. "And I thought Stephanie and Rick were a heavy-duty couple. Did she dump him for Jason just because he can't play soccer?"

"It sure looks like that," I whispered back. "Roger, Rick, and I were in a diner over the weekend, and Stephanie and Jason walked in just as we were leaving. Rick sure seemed surprised. And then Sunday I was over at Rick's, and Jason called. Rick would hardly speak to him."

"Whoa," said Gretchen. "Stop right there. You were *where* yesterday?" Both she and

Amy had leaned forward and were staring at me.

"I was over at Rick's," I explained calmly. "I tried to call you guys last night, but you were away until who knows when. Rick came by the game in Highland yesterday on the way to the hardware store there and invited me over to hear his oldies. It was absolutely unromantic, I promise."

It was true. Early in my visit I had realized that the only way I was going to have any fun was to put my crush on Rick out of my mind and think of him as just another guy. It was the only way I was going to be my real self instead of always trying to imitate the person I thought I should be.

I couldn't explain this to Gretchen and Amy. It was just too uncomfortable. Instead, I skipped all the personal stuff and concentrated on convincing them that Rick and I were just good friends.

"But while we're on the subject of boys," I told them, knowing Amy, at least, could be easily diverted by my information, "I'm trying to encourage Roger to work up the nerve to ask you out, Amy."

"No kidding, really?" she asked, surprised.

"I think he just needs a little encouragement."

"Really?" She was obviously eager for more.

"Yes, really. He told me that he likes you a lot and that he likes to talk to you on the phone. But he was sure you liked Rick better."

"And what did you say?"

"That I was sure you liked Roger better, but I thought it would be a good idea if he got off soccer a little and asked you out to a movie or something."

"And what did he say?" She was getting excited.

"Not much, I'm afraid. Just that he didn't think I was right about his being too involved with soccer, and he didn't say anything at all about asking you out."

"Oh, pooh."

"At least Jenny made the suggestion," Gretchen pointed out. "Maybe he'll give it some thought."

"That's true," agreed Amy. "You never know what might happen."

The week that followed was sensational for me. It was the busiest one I could remember having in a long time.

Monday, Wednesday, and Friday were my soccer practices in Highland Park. I was starting to feel real good about my playing, and I was making friends with the girls on the team.

On Monday I was so exhausted that I fell asleep by mistake when I got home from practice. I felt so refreshed that I got into the short nap routine on Wednesday and Friday as well. Because of a weather foul-up, the North Hollow varsity had its last two games in one week, on Tuesday and Thursday. And I wouldn't have missed them for the world. The Tuesday game against Elwood was an easy win for us because the Elwood boys just weren't very good. I stood on the sidelines while Rick sat at the stat table.

Stephanie was there, too, cheering her loudest for Jason, who apparently listened because he scored four of our six goals. Roger scored the other two.

She gave me one brief nod during the whole game. I was upset to see her standing next to Rick at the table for a while. But I knew from experience that he would really have to keep his mind on the stats and wouldn't have much chance for serious conversation.

During halftime, when Rick got up to stretch his legs, I offered to take over for him in the second half. It wasn't that I wanted to give him the opportunity to hang out with Stephanie. I knew he could use a break.

"Nothing you could say would make me give this job back to you," he joked. "It's just too much fun. Besides," he went on, "I'd rather give the job to someone else and spend the time talking to you."

Was he joking or serious this time? I wished I knew for sure, but Rick's easygoing manner was hard to read.

He recruited Benjamin Firth for the stat table and then came back to talk to me. He wanted to know all about my Monday soccer practice.

As we chatted, I could feel Stephanie's disapproving eyes on me. She stood nearby and stared at us in between shouts of encouragement to Jason. It was a weird feeling. I didn't want to let Stephanie Danworth affect me in any way. And my determination seemed to work because I left that game feeling good about North Hollow's win.

Thursday's game was a lot more tense. The competition, Perth, was a lot stiffer, and the team didn't have such an easy time. After having tied one of our early league games, North Hollow had gone on to win eight. Now word had gotten around that if we won this match, we'd be conference and division champs and be able to go on to the all-state games. Lots of people came out for this final match, including my parents and Erin.

The temperature was decidedly wintery, though the sky was clear and the ground was dry. North Hollow and Perth had identical records, so we were as evenly matched as any teams could be.

Because of this, the scoring stayed painfully low. Stephanie, who started off the game cheering frantically, began to lose steam as the game wore on. Eventually she took on an irritated air, as if the North Hollow boys were ignoring her commands.

While we all stood there cheering and freezing, Rick sat at the stat table patiently recording the plays.

"Your fingers must be frozen," I told him at halftime.

"Just my right hand," he told me, and I noticed that he had pulled a mitten over the fingers on his left hand.

"I'll take the stats over for the second half," I offered. "I've been jumping around, so I'm not nearly so cold as you must be."

"I may just take you up on that offer, Jenny," he answered, "and go inside for a while to warm up."

"Be my guest," I said. "You leave the job in good hands."

"I know that." He smiled as he got up and trotted toward the gym.

So, for the second part of the game, I felt as if I had my old job back as soccer manager. But as I scribbled down all the notations, I realized something very important. With Rick or without him, I was very happy to be me, regular old sophomore Jenny Miller.

Chapter Eleven

It was a happy day in our house when the North Hollow varsity boys' soccer team finished first in their league. They beat Perth 1–0. Roger, as expected, went out of his mind. Because he was so excited, Mom and Dad had given Roger permission to have a victory party at our house over the weekend.

"But you have to do all the work," Dad said.

"And don't go and get Jenny to do it for you," warned Mom. "This is your team and your party." So that meant that Roger was on the phone the whole night inviting everyone over for Saturday night.

Knowing that I was going to be consumed with soccer, both mine and Roger's, over the weekend, I disappeared into my room as soon as dinner was over to get a head start on my weekend homework. For me, it was a quiet, productive evening. I could hear Roger on the phone excitedly inviting all of his friends to the big bash.

When I went down for breakfast the next morning, Roger was already up and on the phone again. "This is going to be the party of the year," he told me when he hung up. "The whole school is coming to celebrate."

Dad, who was reading the paper at the kitchen counter, looked up nervously. "Roger," he said, "just what do you mean by the whole school?"

"Well, the whole squad, that's twenty-five right there, and a lot of guys will bring dates, so that's got to be at least forty."

"If everybody stays well behaved with no funny business, that should just about be OK," said Dad. "But you're going to have to stay on top of the situation. Your mother and I are going to be upstairs, and if things get out of hand, that'll be the end of it." Roger groaned. "Being a host is a lot of work," Dad warned. "And after that bash that Travis Brill threw not that long ago, I can't help being a little apprehensive."

"Everything is going to be just fine," Roger promised. "Besides, I hardly ever see Travis now that he's in college." Travis lives next door, and he had given this huge, noisy party last winter while his parents were away. My parents and some other neighbors complained to the police, and Dad wasn't too thrilled to discover that Roger had been at the party.

When I got to school, Gretchen and Amy were excited about the party, too. Roger had called them both the night before. We spent our free time that day deciding what we were going to wear. By the end of the day I still hadn't decided. Well, I had made two decisions. I would wear something very casual, and it would *not* be a leopard print jump suit.

Saturday morning Mom and Erin drove me to practice in Highland Park while Roger and Dad moved furniture around in the family room for the party that night.

"Erin and I are going shoe shopping, and we'll be back to pick you up," explained Mom as we neared the playing field. Coach Mayall had told us at practice the day before that our Saturday game was cancelled because the other team, Langford, didn't have enough healthy players. Although we were all disappointed, we had voted to have Saturday practice instead.

"Thanks a lot, Mom," I told her as she pulled into a parking space so I could get out.

Practice went smoothly. Everyone was anxious to do well at the next day's game. It was nice to see all those familiar faces, and I realized that I was starting to know all the names of the girls. The sad thing was that there were only three games left in our season. It had only been a week, but I had done a lot of hard playing, and I felt as if I really belonged.

The two-hour practice flew by. Ruth and I walked toward the parking lot with a few other girls who were filling us in on who to look out for at the next day's game.

I didn't actually expect Mom and Erin to be early. Shoe shopping with Erin can be a tedious business. Erin always takes her choices very seriously. She isn't like me, who until recently was satisfied with any old pair of blue running shoes.

Since I wasn't expecting them to arrive on time, I was barely watching the traffic. I hardly noticed the dusty gray station wagon that pulled into the lot.

"Hi, Jenny," Rick said with a big smile as he walked toward me.

"Oh, hi," I said casually.

"I bumped into your mother and Erin down at the shoe store, and they looked like they were having such a good time that I offered to pick you up."

"Really," I answered, completely surprised.

"So how do you like my new shoes?" He

laughed, and I found myself staring at his new blue and white running shoes. "Very nice," I said approvingly. Ruth, Sarah, Janet, and Laina all agreed.

I introduced everyone to Rick, and then we headed for his car. "You really bumped into Mom and Erin?" I questioned him.

"Scout's honor. There's a fifty-percent-off sale down at Winston's, and your sister had a pile of ten shoe boxes in front of her. I saw my chance, and I took it."

"Just what do you mean by that?" I asked.

"I had something else in mind," he confessed.

I looked at him, waiting for an explanation.

"How would you like to drive down to Jones Beach with me? It must be beautiful this time of year."

"It sounds like fun," I answered, but my stomach betrayed me with the most embarrassing rumble.

"I knew you were going to be starved, and I gambled that you were going to be up for the trip, so I went home before I came here and packed up some picnic stuff."

"You think of everything," I told him.

"No, not really. Mostly I think of stomachs."

I climbed into Rick's father's station wagon in my soccer shorts and sweat shirt, carrying my down parka. I had been cold before practice, but now I was too hot to think about wearing it.

"I'm really dressed for the occasion," I joked. And looking over to Rick, I realized that with the exception of his brand-new shoes and a clean face, he was dressed just about as grubbily as I was.

"If you want me to stop by your house so you can get rid of your cleats, I will," he offered. "But promise you won't take time to do a whole number. The days are so short, the sun could be down before we get there."

"Deal," I promised. "But I *am* going to take off my shin guards and knee pads, and wash my face, and put on a pair of jeans. Is there anything else I should get for our picnic?"

"Not a thing."

At home, I ran in and out in five minutes flat. Roger was hard at work at the stove, and the whole place smelled of popcorn.

"I'll be back for dinner," I called to him. "Please tell Mom when she gets back."

Then I jumped back into Rick's car, and we took off for the parkway to Jones Beach.

"Roger is really into this party he's giving tonight," I said. "Are you coming?"

"I suppose." He sounded very unsure.

"It ought to be fun," I said softly and let the subject drop.

The parkway south to Jones Beach was incredibly clear of traffic, and in less than half an hour we were crossing the causeway over Great South Bay on to the strip of land that was Jones Beach. The shrubbery was low, green, and marshy, and the sight of the ocean was overwhelming. It was as if we were entering another world, far from our hectic one.

We went around the traffic circle with the Egyptian-looking monument in the middle. We had seen no more than three or four cars since we had crossed the bridge, but Rick continued to drive past the parking lots, which were completely deserted.

"Where are we going?" I asked finally.

"To the prettiest spot I know out here. It's all the way at the end, and it takes a little longer to get there. I hope you don't mind."

"Not at all," I assured him. "I just don't know much about this place. It's usually so mobbed in the summer that we just hang around at home."

"I know what you mean. We do the same thing, but in the winter it's a different story. Not many people are into visiting a cold beach."

"I guess you can't get much of a tan," I said, and we both laughed.

Ours was the only car on the long, straight road. The bay was on our left, and the ocean, a beautiful sapphire blue, was just visible over the grassy sand dunes on our right. When we finally reached the lot Rick had in mind, he pulled in and parked the car. The sun was warm as I got out of the car, but Rick advised me to take along my parka.

"On the other side of the dunes there's usually a stiff wind," he said as he struggled to fit his cast-covered forearm into the sleeve of his own down jacket.

"Can I give you a hand?" I offered.

"A wrist would be better," he said, laughing. "If you don't mind helping me get the sleeve of this jacket over this lovely hunk of plaster, I'll be able to manage the rest."

"No problem," I said. I timidly tried to slide the jacket over his arm.

"You really have to give it a shove. Don't worry, I won't feel a thing," he assured me.

I felt hesitant about following his directions quite so literally, but after a few more gentle attempts failed, I put a little more muscle into my efforts and finally got the jacket where Rick wanted it. Then I put on my own.

Rick grabbed a red backpack from the car, and we headed across the parking lot to the wooden steps that went over the sand dunes.

"Having second thoughts?" Rick asked as we reached the top of the steps and the cold wind blew into our faces.

"Not at all," I told him. "This is just incredible." The long strip of white sand stretched all the way to the horizon. "I really feel as if we've come to the end of the earth," I told him.

"We have. Come on, I'll show you my favorite spot." We walked together down the deserted beach, our feet sinking into the soft sand. "It gets easier when we reach the hard sand down there," he told me as he pointed to the shoreline. He was right.

We walked for about ten minutes along the water's edge, with sea gulls flying around us and the foamy green surf pounding at the shore. The air was frosty, and I could feel my nose stinging with cold.

Finally we reached a spot where civilization seemed to have disappeared completely. Snack bars, parking lots, stairways, and people were all hidden from view.

Rick motioned to the dunes. "If we head up there, it'll be a little warmer," he told me. "It's probably the best spot for our picnic."

So we left the easy walking of the flat, hard shoreline and trudged through the sand to the base of the dunes, which were protected from hikers with red slatted snow fencing. We were a lot warmer away from the water's edge.

"Don't sit down yet," Rick said as he struggled to pull the zipper open on the backpack. I offered to help, but he waved me away with a laugh. "This is a challenge," he said.

It was like a magician's bag of tricks, it was so full. And as I stood there watching, he pulled out an old sheet for our tablecloth, various packages of cheese, crackers, fruit, a thermos of hot soup, plastic plates, and plastic cups, silverware, and napkins.

"You certainly do things in a big way," I said, much impressed.

"Well, I've never done it before, actually, and I wasn't quite sure what to bring, so I brought along a little of everything."

We were both starved, and we proceeded to eat our way through everything he had brought, talking happily about other great spots that we knew for getting away from it all.

"There's a county wetland and preserve right near North Hollow that hardly anyone knows about called Chataup. Every now and then I ride my bike out there," Rick said.

"I've seen signs for it off Cove Road, but I've never been there."

"It's beautiful. You can really get a feeling for

what North Hollow must have been like before there were any houses and streets."

"I'll have to check it out."

"If you like," said Rick, "we can ride over there together sometime. But it'll have to wait until my wrist is better. Bike riding is one thing I'm not allowed to do right now."

When we finished our lunch, we stowed everything away in the red pack.

"That has to be a lot lighter," I commented as he zipped it up.

"Yeah," he agreed. "Want to build a sand castle?" he asked suddenly.

"Sure, why not," I answered, but I must have sounded doubtful.

"Sand is not just for six-year-olds," he reassured me as we got down on our knees and started pushing mounds of sand toward each other. It didn't take long to build an impressive pile.

"It looks high enough, so just pack down the sides," he instructed.

"You sound as if you have something definite in mind."

"I do," he admitted as we each worked on our own side.

When the castle was neatly packed down, we sat back to admire our work. "Now you are going to see the ultimate sand castle," Rick announced.

Unzipping the red pack once more, he reached down into it and pulled out a green tennis ball. He then began to carve an elaborate path spiraling around the castle, complete with several underground tunnels.

We let the ball roll down it many times, laughing as it jumped its course in various weak spots. Then we had to strengthen the walls or carve the roads deeper. Finally, exhausted from laughing, we sat back on the sand and looked out over the ocean.

"What a great thing," I told him. "I haven't done that since I was little."

We talked about other things that we used to do when we were young, like singing on long car trips and telling knock-knock jokes. We laughed a lot and then realized that the sun had gotten very low in the sky.

"Were you supposed to be home to help Roger?" Rick asked as we trudged back through the sand to the car. I was sad to see the day end, and it sounded like he was, too.

"No, Mom and Dad said that if Roger wanted to have a victory party for the team, he had to do it all by himself. I'm glad I wasn't there because if I had been, I'm sure he would have figured out a way to get me to help. But it's good for him to do it by himself!"

"I agree, especially since it means I don't have to feel guilty about keeping you away from the house all afternoon."

"Hey, I wanted to come," I reminded him.

"And I'm glad you did. It was a great afternoon."

He put his good arm around my shoulder and gave me a big, friendly squeeze and a warm kiss on the cheek. I was so surprised, I thought I would have heart failure right there on the spot. Outwardly, I only laughed, but inside I felt as if someone had dipped me in a tub of cold or hot water and I wasn't sure which.

It was a friendly, brotherly gesture, I thought. When we got back to the car, no more was said about our fun visit to the beach. Instead, we started talking about soccer and the upcoming state championships. And so, with a heavy discussion about soccer, we ended our perfectly fabulous afternoon.

When Rick dropped me at home, I wanted desperately to ask him again whether he was coming to the party. I sensed, though, that it would destroy the bubbly happiness that surrounded us, so I just let him drive away.

Inside our house, Roger had been busy. The

kitchen was filled with bags of potato chips and pretzels and cases of soda.

"Doesn't anyone like to eat anything decent at parties?" I complained to Roger.

"Too much trouble," he told me.

"Cheese and apples aren't hard," I suggested.

"If that's what you want, you do it," he told me.

"Hey, forget it. This is your party, Roger Miller," I told him.

Kids started arriving around eight, and by nine the rec room was jammed. I decided early in the evening that I would be in charge of the music, so I sat comfortably on a couch in a corner, arranging the records that I would play.

Gretchen and Amy arrived early. Amy was having a good time playing darts with Roger and a bunch of other kids, but Gretchen was sitting on one of the couches next to Matt, and both of them looked very uncomfortable.

My sympathy went out to her, but I knew there was nothing I could do to help. After all, I had chosen to hide myself away in the corner with the records rather than have to talk to anyone. After my afternoon with Rick, I only wanted to be with him.

I was sad that he had decided not to come, but I understood his reasons when Jason and

Stephanie arrived, looking very much the royal couple. It would hurt Rick to see them together.

Stephanie was dressed in a shiny turquoise and black jump suit and black high heels, with about a million gold chains around her neck. I wondered why I had ever wanted to look like her. It was because of Rick, I reminded myself as I looked down to see the off-white fuzzy sweater that my mother had bought me. I had on my blue and white striped jeans. I liked what I was wearing, and I couldn't imagine it on Stephanie. It made me feel great to realize that I was finally finding a style of my own.

Nicky and Ted came by and joked with me a little, but then they drifted off to be with other people when they discovered that they couldn't lure me away from my corner.

I got up for a few minutes to change the stack of records. When I was done, I looked across the room to see that Rick had come in. He was wearing jeans and a plaid shirt with one arm rolled up around his cast.

He looked so handsome with a healthy glow from our afternoon on the windy beach.

Stephanie and Jason were standing in the middle of the floor trying to dance with apples on their heads. Roger had taken my suggestion and added apples to his menu at the last minute.

I watched from the safety of my corner as Rick stared at them with an unhappy look on his face. Then he turned away to talk to one of the boys on the team. But within a few minutes, he found his way across the room and sat down on the couch.

"Mind if I join you?" he asked, smiling broadly. He had a sheepish look, something I had never seen on him before.

"Sure," I agreed. "But I'm surprised to see you."

"Well," he started, "I realized it would be silly not to come. I would be cutting off my nose to spite my face, as the saying goes."

"Do you mind explaining what you mean by that, or would you rather keep it a secret?"

"It's a long story," he warned.

"That wouldn't bother me. I've got all night."

"It's really embarrassing," he continued.

"You think you're the only person who's done embarrassing things in his life?" I asked gently.

"No, I guess not."

"Hey, look, this is none of my business," I said, holding up my hand. "Let's forget the whole thing."

"But it is your business," he assured me.

"At least I would like it to be." His voice was timid, and I didn't know what he was getting at.

"OK, Rick. Now you've gone overboard. You have to explain."

"Just give me a minute," he said, laughing. "This has got to be the most awful confession a person could ever make."

"I can't imagine!" I said easily, hoping to reassure him.

"Well, it's Stephanie and Jason," he said in a low voice.

"I know. It must be awful for you to see them together," I finished for him, hoping he would appreciate my understanding.

"Oh, not at all." He chuckled. "I'm relieved to see them together. They're perfect for each other, and Jason has gotten Stephanie off my back."

"What?" It was hard for me to understand what he was saying.

"Stephanie and I had been going together for quite a while, and everyone thought we were the perfect couple, but nothing could have been farther from the truth."

"Rick!" I was shocked.

"It's hard to explain, but I guess I've got to start somewhere." He took a deep breath.

"Stephanie is a very together person. At least she looks and acts it."

"Yes," I agreed.

"And that's what I thought I liked about her. In the beginning it was great to go around with a girl who always knew what she wanted to do. I was so glad to be with her. But now I'm just so glad to get away." I looked at him questioningly because I still wasn't sure what he was getting at.

"Stephanie has this incredible need to look a certain way and be a certain way all the time. And what that means is that she wants to be the center of attention and have everyone do what she likes, go to the parties she wants to go to, hang out at Jo-Jos when she wants to, and go to movies that she wants to see. The worst part of the whole thing is that what Stephanie wants to do always involves hordes of people. I like to hang out as well as the next person, but Stephanie *never* wants to do anything without a crowd."

"I don't understand *that*!" I exclaimed involuntarily.

"I think it's kind of hard to be the center of attention when there are only two of you," he said, and I could feel a hint of humor in his tone. "Anyway, I've been trying to break it off with her as gently as I could, but she refused to take a hint. She even tried to get Jason to help her." Then he laughed. "Except, there was no way he could help. We're just too different and not at all suited for each other. I wasn't going to come tonight because, honestly, I'm really sick of going to parties with Stephanie. It hasn't been fun for a long time."

"Well, from a purely selfish point of view," I blurted out, "I'm glad you came. You're about the only person I felt like talking to."

"I'm glad I came, too," he admitted, reaching over and taking my hand. My first instinct was to pull it away, because after my own confession, the last thing I could stand was brotherly comfort.

But I left my hand in his, and to my surprise, I found that instead of a quick, friendly squeeze, Rick was holding my hand softly and firmly in his own.

"I came to be with you," he said, his beautiful gray eyes searching my face. "You're something special, Jenny. You're the girl I thought Stephanie would be. It just took me a little while to realize it."

I felt myself overcome with a kind of happiness that I had never felt before, and I pressed his hand back. "If you only knew, Rick, what I've been through."

"Whatever it was, it seems to have agreed with you."

"Now it's my turn to be embarrassed," I said, and I knew I was turning bright red. But I knew if I could tell Rick about it, I would feel a lot better.

He removed his hand from mine only to put his arm around my shoulder. I snuggled in closely and sighed.

"This is definitely the right time for confessions," he told me. "So let's have it before you lose your nerve like I almost did."

"You?"

"Sure. If I had stayed home, I could have hidden out in my room all night and never said a word. And now look where it's gotten me." With that, he leaned his face toward mine. I had never kissed anyone before, but I knew that kissing Rick Henley was the nicest, most special thing I had ever done. It was so tender and reassuring. I wished it would go on forever.

I was reminded of my horrible date with Jason. I started to laugh as we continued to kiss each other softly.

"What's so funny?" Rick whispered.

"Forgive me, but I'm thinking about Jason."

"What about him?" Rick pulled back, suddenly worried.

"That night we went to the dance, he wanted to kiss me, but I couldn't do it. I really wanted to kiss you."

"Really?" He sounded so pleased. "Is that what you were going to confess?"

"There's a little more," I admitted. "But it's about Stephanie." I was quiet after that because I just didn't know what to say next.

"Let's have it." He smiled. "I have a feeling we're on the same wavelength."

"It's just that I thought that if I dressed like she did, you'd realize I wasn't just a kid anymore."

"I noticed all right," he told me. "I noticed there was another flashy girl around. But by then, I had learned my lesson. I wasn't going to get trapped again."

"Rick, I'm crushed," I complained.

"Sorry," he joked, but then turned serious. "Something must have happened when you made the Highland soccer team, because all of a sudden you seemed different. You opened up, and I began to realize how terrific you were. But it wasn't until today at the beach that I knew for sure. I can't remember having had such a good time with anyone—ever."

"Me, either," I said.

"And I can't wait to go out to Chataup with

you. If you want to go with me, that is," he added, quickly looking very concerned.

I was amazed to see that he had no idea how I really felt, but the smile I gave him set the record straight. "I happen to know a couple of great spots myself," I assured him.

"I have a feeling we'll find a lot of places to visit and things to do together," he said. "Although I bet we'll have a good time wherever we go. You just seem like that kind of person."

I sighed contentedly as he rubbed his soft cheek against mine. Just then, Stephanie let out a strangled screech, and we looked over to see that she and Jason were dancing with apples in their mouths as well as on their heads.

"They make a cute couple, don't you think," said Rick. "But then, so do we."

I had to agree.

EXCITING NEWS FOR ROMANCE READERS

Love Letters—the all new, hot-off-the-press Romance Newsletter. Now you can be the first to know:

What's Coming Up:
* Exciting offers
* New romance series on the way

What's Going Down:
* The latest gossip about the SWEET VALLEY HIGH gang
* Who's in love . . . and who's not

Who's Who:
* The real life stories about SWEET DREAMS cover girls
* The true facts about SWEET DREAMS authors

Who's New:
* Meet Kelly Blake
* Find out who's a *Winner* And much, much more!

Fill out this coupon, mail it in, and this spring your free copy of *Love Letters* is on its way to you. *Love Letters*—you're going to love it.

Please send me my free copy of Love Letters

Name _____ Age _____

Address _____

City _____ State _____ Zip _____

To: BANTAM BOOKS
Dept. KR
666 Fifth Avenue
New York, NY 10103

SD6—2/86

THIS EXCITING NEW SERIES IS ALL ABOUT THE THREE MOST ENVIED, IMITATED AND ADMIRED GIRLS IN MIDVALE HIGH SCHOOL: STACY HARCOURT, GINA DAMONE AND TESS BELDING. THEY ARE WINNERS—GOLDEN GIRLS AND VARSITY CHEERLEADERS—YET NOT EVEN THEY CAN AVOID PROBLEMS WITH BOYFRIENDS, PARENTS, AND LIFE.

☐ **THE GIRL MOST LIKELY (WINNERS #1) 25323/$2.25**

Stacy Harcourt is the captain of the varsity cheerleading squad, but she wants to break from her rigid, boring image as "Miss Perfect." But in doing so will she lose the friendship of Gina and Tess and the captainship of the squad? Or will she realize that maybe her "perfect" life wasn't so bad after all. 25323/$2.50

☐ **THE ALL AMERICAN GIRL (WINNERS #2)25427/$2.25**

Gina Damone has problems keeping up socially with the other cheerleaders because of her immigrant parents old-world attitudes. But when she begins dating All-American Dex Grantham his breezy disregard for her parents' rules makes her question his sincerity.

THE GOOD LUCK GIRL (WINNERS #3)

Cute, cuddly Tess Belding is the first student from Midvale's vocational-technical program ever to make the cheering squad, but she's going to be benched unless she can pass her French midterm! *Coming in May 1986.*

SWEET DREAMS are fresh, fun and exciting,—alive with the flavor of the contemporary teen scene—the joy and doubt of *first love*. If you've missed any SWEET DREAMS titles, from #1 to #100, then you're missing out on *your* kind of stories, written about people like *you!*

Prices and availability subject to change without notice.